For those we lost to the darkest shadows.

You will be with us, always.

X

ALSO AVAILABLE– CITY OF RED… BY COLIN A. MAY.

A NOTE FROM THE AUTHOR.

This book continues to explore the City of Red. A collection of eleven new tales, throughout different times in the city. I considered placing the stories in chronological order but felt it may give the impression that each tale builds one story, much like my first book. Although all eleven tales are set in the same city, they each have a life of their own, each one has its own purpose.

Whilst writing this book, I acquired the help of some extraordinary artists who created their own visions inspired by each tale. Please take the time to admire the excellent works found inside these pages and be sure to research each artist and devour their many incredible creations.

A huge thanks must go out to Anita Hunt, who took on the daunting task of editing and proofreading my work... the skills and guidance she has offered me helped shape and grow my vision further than before.

I hope you enjoy these tales and continue to find the light hidden in the darkness.

Contents

City of Red *TALES*

Seven String Killer

1

Carly's fingers worked a perfectly timed dance around the fret board, picking out a sequence of notes that provided the technically beautiful soundtrack to her morning. The reverberations from the seven strings hastily fed the triple pickups with a ferocious anger which was frantic, yet beautifully elegant. Electric currents fuelled the powerful amplifier with the music's jubilant energy. A pair of acoustically brilliant loudspeakers regurgitated the sound, agitating the thick walls of Carly's apartment. The music she created was from the heart, a heart thought to be cold and black... incapable of any feeling. Only a tight pocket of people truly knew the real Carly, few were capable of accurately dissecting her personality... she struggled to allow anyone to get too close. Instead of socialising, she preferred to live her days in a quiet, solitary mindset, surrounded by the sounds of her music... her perfect solution to block out the chaos of the city. Her introvert nature meant a huge chunk of her personality was locked away from prying eyes. When she played, her heart opened, releasing the pressurised cap on her carefully guarded emotions. The release injected her music with extra soul and passion.

Cuttings from various comic books decorated the apartment with a mosaic of colour littered with speech bubbles and bold captions. The displays of such graphical literature projected her love for superheroes in a flourish of vibrancy which many may see as immature, reminiscent of a bedroom decorated by a carefree child... but there was a meticulously sophisticated feel to the apartment that mimicked the personality of its inhabitant. Thin strips of neon lighting, tucked into the gloss-black mouldings lining the ceiling's perimeter, provided the room with a glow which could be altered by the user at any time, both in colour and in brightness, by a simple spoken command. Behind the comic-cuttings, barely visible beneath the boxes of cartoonish action scenes, the walls were painted in a soft shade of magenta. Irregular purple specks scattered amongst the deep pile of the otherwise black carpet were complimented by the hidden colour of the interior walls. The ceiling was predominantly a brilliant white, but it borrowed many other colours from the neon-lights surrounding it. The décor in her apartment also seemed to pair with the elated, yet heavy, rock music obliterating the silence of her solitary lair each day. When she played, Carly's mind was in silence, her thoughts were at peace. Despite her meticulous routines and her focused mind, she regularly allowed herself little pockets of time to play - her music was her release from the violence in her day to day living.

She kept a mindful eye on the hands of the antique, mahogany grandfather clock which stood proudly by the entrance to the kitchen. The clock was slim in form, picturesque in design, an heirloom passed down by an old mentor. Time was a precise factor that needed to be constantly assessed, not nervously or with any hint of panic, just enough to keep the rigid schedule that Carly felt to be imperative to her lifestyle.

Heavy mechanical gears jolted the hour hand forward, declaring the time at one o'clock: time to get to work.

Carly tapped the transmitter switch on her electric guitar, muting the speakers before springing from her stool. The seven-string guitar sparkled under a bright blue light mounted in the ceiling. A million miniscule flecks of gold, embedded in the green v-shaped body, caught the attention of the overhead lighting array. The gold flecks seemed to ripple in a glorious wave of inanimate life as glossy reflections travelled the body's length before the guitar found its home, holstered amongst the comic book cuttings on the wall. Carly threw a small shoulder bag over her right shoulder then snatched up a black briefcase from the floor, along with a slim, dark-purple guitar case. She scanned the living room, performing a final check, ensuring everything had been returned to its correct position - everything was in order, neatly tucked away and set in place.

'Front door, open!' she barked to the voice activated control system.

A sharp tonal bleep of acknowledgement filled the apartment as the front door slides open.

'Systems, shutdown!' her second order commenced the power-down procedure of the non-essential electrical devices, and the room fell into darkness.

The gentle hum of electrical circuitry ceased as the apartment's pulsating life source became dormant.

The streets were swarming with the usual rush-hour foot traffic: the Donningtown area, famed for being a hive of activity, full of wealthy, often powerful and influential inhabitants, was as crammed and claustrophobic as the rest of the city. Only the privileged few could afford to be seen in a place like this, let alone take up residence in the luxury apartments standing at the end of a three-year long waiting list. The wealth in Donningtown could never guarantee a calm or relaxed atmosphere... and it certainly didn't guarantee manners and considerate behaviour either. There was a definite feeling of dog eat dog amongst the residents, and Carly was no exception.

She marched down the street with an impolite and brash urgency, bumping shoulders with her co-inhabitants who shared her lack of care for the fellow man. She ducked and weaved, squeezing through the bustle of unfriendly faces. Her thoughts were focused, she knew her destination and she knew her goal... she wasn't going to let anyone delay her precisely timed schedule.

Donningtown's Sky-rail system was a few minutes from her home and the means for her route across the city. It was the perfect mode of transport for Carly: always punctual, timed to the minute, and could be accessed with an untraceable paper ticket, a rarity and novelty in the city's advanced technological climate.

Her methodical, almost robotic eyes busily scanned the Sky-rail station. With meticulous efficiency, her brain examined the haze of bodies, searching for any familiar faces to avoid.

...Assessment complete: platform clear of threat.

She stepped aboard the first carriage on the platform. Two automatic doors silently closed behind her in a smooth, elegant motion. A surge of energy cracked through the overhead rails and the twenty-three carriages accelerated towards the heart of the city.

The carriage was alive with busy commuters lost in conversations with their various communication devices - plugged in and zoned out from the world around them, lost in their own, carefree little bubbles. Carly checked the communicator strapped to her wrist: it beeped and flashed the current time, confirming the Sky-rail was in-line with her schedule.

A mixture of metals and carbon-fibre composites cocooned the passengers in engineless carriages propelled by powerful electrical currents surging through the rails beneath them. The gallery of windows in each carriage were useless once the shuttle was at full speed, as the city's scenery blitzed past the plasti-cote windows in a single, continuous streak of light. Despite the transport's efficient high speeds, the Sky-rail's passengers travelled in comfort with the aid of a complex stabilising wizardry that Carly gave up trying to explain to her inquisitive little sister. Elza was twelve years old, and by chance the siblings shared the same birthday. Being nineteen years younger and possessing a mind hungry for information, she was about as annoying as any younger sister could possibly be...

Carly dreaded Elza's unannounced visits. Their mother would drop the child off without any prior communications... she would just stand at the door, leaning on the buzzer, with the assumption Carly would be available for spontaneous childcare duty. As soon as the young girl entered Carly's apartment, her hands would be over everything, with no respect for precious belongings. It drove Carly insane and was the cause of many debates with the child about crossing one's personal boundaries. Every time Carly boarded the Sky-rail, she would be reminded of her endless questions about the mechanics of the city's efficient transportation system, conversations which would undoubtedly end up in the loss of

Carly's usually well-kept temper.

Startlingly, a gentle tap on her shoulder disrupted her from the melancholy dream of stressful interactions with Elza.

She turned her head a quarter turn, examining a tall, hulking man... she could almost feel the condensation from his breath.

'Hey, sugar? Where do you get off?' he grunted through a shiny set of pearl-white teeth. The man smiled widely and winked in a playful, cheeky manner, trying to soften his poor attempt of flirting.

Placing her guitar case on the carriage floor, Carly allowed her instincts to guide her next movements.

She slowly rotated her body to face her fellow commuter. A swift, powerful squeeze of her left hand brought the towering man to her eye level. She grinned as a pair of large testicles scrunched together in her tight grip.

'Speak to me again, fucker, and you won't ever be getting off.' She spoke softly, yet with an assertive tone that confirmed her intent to do serious damage if pushed. 'Do we have an understanding, buddy?'

The 6ft 5, well-turned-out man writhed awkwardly in pain, contorting his legs in a futile attempt to rise over his 5ft 5 attacker. Their eyes remained fixed in a disturbing moment of contentment.

'Yeah, fuck! Jeez, I get you... fuck. Shit, lady! Please...' he begged, 'please let go? You got my balls!'

Despite the hulking commuter dwarfing Carly with his impressive physical build, he knew she had the upper hand in the situation... she had him quite literally by the balls.

He could feel, almost smell, the sweat pouring from his forehead as other commuters began to take notice of his panicked state.

'I am glad we have reached an amicable agreement here, Sugar!' She tightened her grip for a few seconds.

Her hand still gripped tightly, she gave him a small, determined smile. The expression spoke a thousand words... but there were four very prominent words which stood out over the rest. Four assertive words which left an imprint across the network of his mind... *'Don't fuck with me!'* The dangerous glint in her eye also preached an identical warning that could not be taken lightly.

The commuter tried to calm himself, sedating the aggression beginning to boil within his soul.

He was desperate to explode, ready to engage...

He imagined tearing Carly apart with his bare hands.... but an inner voice begged him not to try his luck... it pleaded with him to see reason.

Carly's bold approach and words of warning sang a song of confidence needing to be heard. He was perplexed by her sterile demeanour - her face was full of focus and unreadable of any kind of emotion.

Carly's grin widened, her grip loosened slightly, and her fingers began to toy with the commuter's burning testicles. She rolled his genitals around in her hand, rubbing them against each other, almost soothing them. Her cold eyes remained locked with his but, despite the grin, she remained expressionless.

He struggled to get a grip on the unfolding situation, his already confused and panicked mind went to work trying to analyse her actions. His lips buckled and contorted in cartoonish confusion.

Carly was unknown to him, his first interaction with her was just a playful bit of flirting on his part, allured by her braided, blonde locks, but the response he received had been threatening to his health - potentially damaging to his manhood. Then followed the uncomfortably forward and playful groping of his tenderised genitals... Carly's actions were truly baffling and extremely unnerving to him.

Tension began to build in his designer jeans as Carly's fingers started to arouse him. A large lump lodged in the middle of his throat. Heavier beads of sweat began to form on his brow, dominating the first wave of perspiration.

Carly's stare became more intense. Her smile twisted, transforming into a snarl which displayed the first signs of any real emotion on her part: contempt.

The point of a sharp needle stabbed into his neck, interrupting the collective of confused sexual images beginning to rapidly clutter in his mind. A stream of cold fluid rushed into his veins and attacked his body, instantly paralysing him.

He dropped to the floor in a comfortable heap, numb to the world. His body relaxed, his eyes rolled back, and his brain went to sleep.

Carly stepped backwards, picked up her guitar case and turned to ignore the sedated man. She discreetly placed the used syringe back into the pocket of her small shoulder bag.

Her actions, her defensive assault, had all been precisely timed and swiftly executed to assure maximum discretion. A small number of her fellow commuters looked on in curiosity at the fallen man, but nobody seemed particularly concerned by his sudden tiredness... just another random event of the daily commute for many.

Carly stood calmly, her focus unaltered by the event.

Two doors opened in front of Carly in a smooth, elegant motion and she casually stepped out from the carriage.

Clusters of fellow commuters found themselves in a confused, agitated tangle as they impatiently concerned themselves with their personal agendas. One group fought to board the carriage behind her, with a brutish, unapologetic urgency. Whilst the other group barged their way from the transport and onto the platform, keen to scurry around the city in their own hectic scamper.

The rest of the station was just as noisy and chaotic as the boarding platform... alive with the usual city mayhem. The hustlers were bawling out their entertaining words of joy as they showcased their cheap parlour tricks to the weary, uninterested masses. Announcements of shuttle arrivals echoed and faded amongst the general population. Constant, inane chatter droned on through the muggy air. The occasional cries and high-pitched screams of a hungry young babe pierced through all the murmurs of commotion.

Carly's brain went into scan-mode once again, collecting

information from her surroundings and the mass of faces around her…

…Assessment complete.

The station was clear of any concerns and abnormalities, she was safe to set off. She always checked her surroundings… always preparing for the unexpected.

Her stride was powerful, full of intent. Her long, silver dress rippled against her body in a super-slow motion as she placed one foot in front of the other. She held her head high, keeping her posture strong and confident. She snapped her neck to the left, tossing her braided, blonde locks down her back…

…She was ready to take on another new day in the heart of the city.

2

The sweat seeping from John's unhealthily pale skin began to sizzle under the mid-morning sun. The atmosphere in the city was always thick with pollution and the humidity was often a struggle for most, but simply unbearable for many others.

The searing heat claimed hundreds of lives throughout an average year. The infamous 'City Sweat', a few years before, had claimed the lives of over one-hundred-thousand civilians in extreme weather conditions which pushed residents far beyond their physical limits. The catastrophe shook the world and was poignant enough for John to begin his detailed studies of the city's dense, polluted climate.

John Sharrd specialised in the effects of the city's atmospheric pollutants upon the human body. His studies often caused controversy and upset amongst government officials, with his claims of undeniable links between the city's pollution levels and the aggressive spread of human mutations found in many citizens dwelling in the thickest smog of the city. The mutations monitored by John never gave anyone the power of flight or the ability to burn through walls with a concentrated stare, but there were signs of enhanced strength and higher pain thresholds than would be deemed normal. Visible body mutations were also apparent, but many believed they were linked to a nuclear reactor leak which had gone unnoticed for almost a decade.

Countless government officials tried to put an end to John's work and dismiss his 'radical' claims, but his studies received the backing of a wealthy technology company, primarily involved in developing air-conditioning units which claimed to 'filter and neutralise' many of the city's toxins. With large financial backing behind John's work, the government officials tried to publicly discredit John in numerous ways - often personally. After an expensive smear campaign, aimed to discredit his work, failed to silence him, John was arrested for the crime of necrophilia. It was claimed: after the heart breaking and costly breakdown of his long-term marriage, he had begun to sexually interfere with the human corpses he had obtained for his studies. John's financial backers poured vast amounts of money into a lengthy battle to clear his name and keep the remnants of his reputation intact. A high-cost legal team fought tirelessly to rid all claims raised against him… and succeeded.

In the aftermath, several officials from the Mayor's Office and the Police Department faced their own charges. Many were given lengthy prison sentences for their involvement in manufacturing the evidence used to frame John Sharrd.

The publicity from the smear campaign and the subsequent unearthing of the scandals which followed, propelled John's public image and reputation to unprecedented levels. Investors rejoiced, ensuring his funds would never run dry and his work would receive all the backing he could ever need.

John played with the synthetic scrambled eggs on the plate in front of him, watching the yellowish, gelatine-like substance wobble with every jab and poke from his fork. The substance looked like it was supposed to, it moved like it was supposed to, but the taste was strange. It left a strong and unusual tang in the mouth which could only be described as unnatural, yet not quite nauseating. He had cleared away the toast and synthi-pork with ease, enjoying every mouthful, but the eggs were proving to be a real battle of will and dedication. Despite John's stomach nagging at him, reminding him of his hunger, the eggs just weren't appetising. It had been decades since he had tasted real eggs, but his memory was true enough to remind him that the synthetic substitute served to him, was nothing but a poor imitation.

As the scrambled mess wobbled on his plate, a bead of sweat left the tip of his nose and landed in the middle of the remaining breakfast.

John screwed up his face, placed his knife and fork on the plate and pushed the meal to the side of the table in revulsion - *as if these eggs weren't already off-putting?* he thought to himself.

A keen, chirpy waitress swiftly approached the table. She

displayed a child-like bounce in her stride, and her face was a ray of sunshine which appeared to be from natural happiness, not the usual strained pretend smile that many in her profession often wore. A sweet fragrance clung to the air around her - probably from a cheap bottle of perfume purchased with scratchings from the meagre wage offered by a waitressing role, but it was a sweet and pleasant fragrance, nonetheless.

The waitress leaned forward over John's table. She cupped her hands together and asked if he had enjoyed his food. John's forced smile and a gentle nod was enough to satisfy the gleeful waitress. He leaned back in his chair, quietly composed, watching her clear the table. Once she had finished, she left a complimentary packet of three brightly coloured biscuits in front of him. The gesture confused him... *she had already cleared away the empty mug that once contained an agreeable milky tea. If she had given him a top-up, the packet of biscuits would have been the perfect accompaniment.*

John brushed aside the biscuits, along with his confusion, before glancing at the orange and black watch wrapped around his wrist: 13:36, time to get to the office.

An array of red lights criss-crossed in uniform patterns beneath the colourless glass flooring. The lighting design had a low output, intended only to create a slight, tranquil glow through the office, whilst complementing the rest of the room's lighting and décor. Large mirrors panelled the walls floor to ceiling. Each mirror separated by a miniscule beading of light which changed colour every thirty seconds in a pulsating motion, from red to blue, blue to green, green to red, and so on. The ceiling, finished in high-gloss black, was by far the most distracting part of the office: it looked alive with its scattering of white lights, gently flickering on and off, designed to resemble a galaxy of twinkling stars in the night. Four large glass tables took centrepiece of the room, each had a slight tint of dark green throughout their construction. The whole room was sterilised twice a day by a dedicated team of four. The office's cabinets and drawers were discreetly masked behind the mirrored panels, each one meticulously organised and only accessible by the voice activated computer system operating throughout the office. The system's creator had granted it the name of 'Zeena', programmed only to obey the orders of authorised users. The system worked effectively for the most part... but could be a problematic nuisance when it failed to recognise even the simplest of commands.

John always thought of his own office as 'flash', far too flamboyant for his tastes and requirements - yet it was nothing compared to this room: the office of his backer and sponsor, Arnold Tames.

The room was kept at a constant 18 degrees Celsius and utilised the company's technology in air-conditioning to ensure only the cleanest, purest oxygenated air circulated through the system. Zeena monitored the atmosphere in the office constantly and adjusted the filtration system according to any contaminations or inconsistencies which occurred. Zeena's coding was complex and her operations were more advanced than required for an average office control system, yet she was not A.I. She had no ability to think freely, only follow orders and programming.

'Zeena?' John called out.

'Hello, Mr Sharrd. How may I be of assistance?' Zeena spoke in a robotic, emotion-free tone.

'I am due to meet with Arnold, any idea where he is? It's not like him to be late!' John paced through the office, checking his pale and gaunt reflection in the mirrors, his steps turning into a short, poorly choreographed dance he had once seen in an old movie.

'I am unable to locate his position, Mr Sharrd. The GPS in his bracelet is currently unavailable - possibly caused by electronic interference from another device close to his proximity, or it could be a simple malfunction. Do you require me to call his communicator?'

'Yes, that would be the best solution. Thank you, Zeena.' John always found himself communicating with Zeena with a dull robotic tone, mimicking the one it had been given by its creator. He didn't know why, but it was the same scenario when he conversed with people with foreign accents, it was an uncontrollable habit which he wasn't aware of, until after the fact.

Arnold Tames' office was situated on the 270th floor, the building's uppermost storey, just above the thickest smog clouding the city. John watched out of the huge office window, trying to create a picture of the streets below, but they were a long way down and the smog was too thick to make out anything other than glimpses of movement and glimmers of light from the eternally illuminated city.

'Perhaps one day...' John paused and let out an audible sigh, '...this city will be clear of all this pollution? Perhaps we are all doomed? Have we gone too far with all our needs to colonise and feed from the planet's resources? Where will we end up?' John asked himself, as he looked down on the city.

'I am sorry, I do not understand your request. How may I be of assistance, Mr Sharrd?' Zeena questioned.

'No, no! It wasn't a request, Zeena. I was merely contemplating life, thinking aloud... but errm, thank you! Tell me, did you have any success with Arnold's communicator?'

'I am afraid that I did not, Mr Sharrd. I have sent a beacon to his communicator, it requests for him to get in contact as soon as he is able to do so. Do not worry, I am sure he is fine and dandy!'

Fine and dandy, a phrase John had not heard for many years until he met Arnold's artificial office assistant, and even before that, he did not recall hearing the words often. Each time Zeena said 'fine and dandy', it alerted John to the unusual choice of phrase. He wondered if it was something the system's creator used regularly or if it was a phrase somehow learned by Zeena at some point - *unlikely as it was not artificial intelligence,* he thought to himself. Zeena's learning capabilities, if any, were far beyond comprehension.

John observed himself in the wall of mirrors, examining his reflection - he had lost a lot of weight in a short number of months and barely recognised himself. The skin was hanging from his bones, his once chubby build had transformed into a malnourished skeleton that would not look out of place on a cold, concrete slab in the morgue. He promised himself a visit to the company's med-bay by the end of the week - the same promise he had been making for the last month or more.

Arnold Tames' absence from the office was not uncommon, he lived a busy lifestyle and would often miss meetings, especially with John. Despite the great financial support his work received from the company, John knew he was never a high priority during Tames' hectic, daily schedule. The backing provided for his research was never conditional to constant progress updates, which suited John - allowing him plenty of breathing space and a great sense of freedom in his work.

John had arranged the meeting with his backer to report on some new, possibly troubling findings which would finally give them the opening for legal proceedings against the government. It would prove not only their negligence, but also their involvements in the city's high pollution levels, resulting in rapidly increasing numbers of mutating civilians. John Sharrd's agenda was personal, Arnold Tames' agenda was financial: a legal case could win the company some high value contracts. John knew this, and he knew he needed Arnold and his company to grant him every bit of backing they could. They were planning to engage in a brutal legal war with the city's corrupt government, not an easy task. His already troubling experience taught him more casualties were inevitable in the fallout, and he knew he needed some heavy backup.

'Mr Sharrd, I have received a communication! You are required on the roof where Mr Tames' helicopter will soon be arriving' announced the office's assistant.

'The roof? Why?' John scanned the cityscape, searching for an approaching helicopter.

'I do not have the relevant information to provide an adequate answer to your question, Mr Sharrd, I am afraid that is all I have for you.'

'He must be on a tight schedule. I guess this will be another short meeting then?' John hurried across the polished glass of the office floor - his thin, stringy legs catching the glow of the under-floor lighting, creating an almost strobing effect as he passed each one in turn. His shoes squeaked with every rushed step, a sound that brought a childish smile to his face.

John could be a profoundly serious man, but like many people he harboured an inner child who begged to come out.

'Please do not hurry, do not panic... I am sure everything will be fine and dandy' requested Zeena as she opened the office door for John's exit.

3

The early afternoon sun, having risen from its infancy, pierced through the dense, toxic smog. A fierce, blistering heatwave scorched the city with a brutal and relentless efficiency. Regardless of the mass of pollutants choking the city air, the noxious clouds were incapable of neutralising the power of the abominable summer.

The exterior of the Yachtsman Plaza greedily absorbed a wealth of the sun's rays, distributing the radiant energy through the metal compounds used in the vessel's magnificent construction.

The Yachtsman Plaza: a purpose-built cruise liner situated in the heart of the city. The ship's sole design was to serve as a super-sized collective of luxury restaurants, catering for only the richest of the city's residents. The Yachtsman had never been on a voyage. It had never even seen the ocean and was constructed solely for effect - to serve the high-browed posers with extra-deep wallets and the necessity to fill their lives with the warmth of status symbols. Each deck offered a different atmosphere, a different team employed to serve, a different décor, a different feel. With each level of the ship you climbed, the more substantial your bragging rights... and the higher the service charge became.

The Yachtsman Plaza: famous worldwide for luxury cuisine from the finest chefs, who often lived outlandish lifestyles with their obscene wage packets. Patrons always tipped generously - it was expected of them. If a patron failed to leave a tip, their chances of securing a future table reservation were slim to non-existent. In turn, the status symbol they had secured upon making a reservation would transform into an inescapable mark of shame.

The Yachtsman Plaza: home to the city's most valuable collection of artworks, proudly placed on display throughout the cruise-liner. The highest deck, simply named 1st Class, showcased the finest collection of the whole ship. Each painting displayed upon the walls of the 1st Class dining area dwarfed the collective price of the most beautifully crafted meals from the city's premier kitchens. The sculptures placed amongst the dining tables had been painstakingly created from the world's rarest materials. Each example of art widely considered to be a true marvel to behold. Even the tableware showcased fine artwork, formed from the most exclusive metals known to man.

The Yachtsman Plaza: equipped with one of the most up to date security systems on the market, with a sophisticated satellite array mounted on a large spire of twisting metals. The satellites relayed the liner's status in real-time to a specialised company privileged with direct contact with the city's busy police department. The global security firm also had their own armed units, authorised to use considerable force when necessary, a matter often questioned in the public courts.

The Yachtsman Plaza: the prime location to be seen when in need of an alibi. However, if you were even spotted on-board the obscenely sized restaurant, never would the term 'needle in a haystack' be so apt - huge express elevators and miles of winding escalators throughout assisted both the staff and the patrons to navigate the huge vessel. Once a table was acquired however, simply having one's name on the reservation list was the type of alibi that was rarely questioned

Reserving a table was always a challenging task, despite the liner's gargantuan size and seating capacity… but as ever, money is always a great bargaining chip - there was always someone lurking in the shadows, waiting with eager, sweaty palms.

Carly carved her juicy steak into small, manageable chunks, each one almost identical to the last. The edges of the steak which could not be neatly dissected into uniform cubes, were carved into smaller portions and placed at the side of her plate, folded into a thick, creamy cheese and garlic sauce. Apart from the eighteen ounce, medium-rare beef steak and the generous helping of sauce, the rest of the large plate was barren, free from any accompanying steamed vegetables or salad. The beautifully glazed, white, oval-shaped plate rested on a deep-red heat mat, ensuring the meal was kept at an optimum temperature for consumption. This was the third time Carly had dined at the Yachtsman. The third time she had ordered the steak with cheese and garlic sauce. The third time she had quietly sat alone at table 0961. The third time she had used The Yachtsman Plaza for her delicate business needs. Carly wasn't so much a creature of habit, more of a stickler for routines and planning. A level of precise and structured planning for which she had been praised highly amongst the others in her profession.

Carly took the time to enjoy her meal, taking delight in every satisfying bite. To the unsuspecting eye, she had no care in the world. She just focused on methodically eating her way through the thick, tender steak and gloriously creamy sauce.

Carly felt comfortable dining alone, she felt that she had always been alone, even when surrounded by others.

The only recollection Carly had of her childhood, was her father saying 'Girl, you better learn to fend for yourself, because you aren't going to get a man with that face'... a less than charming remark, one which nagged her shattered memory.

To say Carly was unattractive would be unfair. She was physically fit and looked after her body well. Two large birthmarks on the left of her face had left her looking as though she had been attacked by a blade and now wore the scars. The marks were not visible from a distance and Carly had learned to be comfortable with them, but in her younger days, with a little persuasion from the memories of her father's words, she had once considered surgery. She even attended a couple of consultations. The medics told her she would be completely free of her birthmarks and nobody would ever know. They told her she would feel 'gorgeous'. The medics' words had only enraged her... Carly already felt gorgeous in her own skin. Throughout her life, she had always been confused with the need to conform with how society believes a woman should look. 'Fuck them... and fuck the image of a perfect woman'.

Once her meal was finished and the plate meticulously cleaned, she checked the timings to her schedule. She allowed herself a few more minutes of peace and savoured the lasting flavours swimming across her palate. A brief moment of meditation followed, clearing her mind in preparation for the tasks ahead.

Carly quietly hailed the attention of the waiter who presented a delicate gold threaded envelope. She paid the bill, leaving the obligatory, generous tip tucked away into the pre-folded compartment of the envelope.

A nagging feeling of curiosity struck her and taunted her for a few seconds. She stared at the uniformed digital pictures replicating a wall of porthole windows, designed to create a sense of The Yachtsman being ocean bound. It was hard to fathom why anyone would make the decision to build a cruise liner in the middle of the city, but they had. She searched her memories for details of the owners of the cruise liner, but no names came to mind... *perhaps it was a consortium who financed the project? After all, the initial financial outlay for such a colossal construction must have been horrific*? Carly had travelled the world extensively, but she had never experienced another restaurant like the Yachtsman Plaza. *Could it be one of a kind?*

Carly ran her fingers across her lips, reminded herself of the purpose of meditation and removed herself from her thoughts. She reached under the table and gathered her bags, before heading for the exit.

Passing through the restaurant, amongst the other patrons, she made a point of making prolonged eye contact with a scattering of wandering eyes. She had to ensure her presence at The Yachtsman Plaza was encapsulated in the back of any curious minds.

The city heat hit her hard upon exiting the restaurant. The high temperature was not something Carly welcomed, especially when mixed with the unpleasant humidity. She felt the sweat exude from her pores almost as soon as she left the comfort of the air-conditioned, luxury liner. The unpleasant sticky feeling on her face was second to the displeasure she felt from the lines of oozing perspiration chasing down her back.

The offensive heat reminded her of the 'Feed the Sun' movement who had been campaigning across the city for almost a decade. In a random chain of events, Bobby Lexmark, an unknown face amongst the world, happened upon a television film crew. The investigative crew were travelling the streets, interviewing city inhabitants about their thoughts on rising pollution levels. Rather than opening into a rant about the decline of the atmosphere, Bobby went on camera and praised the polluted air for 'fuelling his body with SHAZAM'. Without any logical explanation of what Shazam was, he had started a brand-new movement and unwittingly became the leader and founder of a dedicated cult who rapidly became a common sight on the city streets. Carly had never understood why anyone would praise elevated levels of pollution, but amid a soaring heatwave, the Feed the Sun movement were always out in force, worshipping the wretched polluted climate. Carly hoped she didn't happen upon the crazed cult today, as they would always summon high levels of media and public attention.

A short walk from The Yachtsman Plaza, Carly positioned herself in the perfect location to capture an unobstructed view over the heart of the city. The rooftop of the Lifestyle News building rose 287 storeys into the sky - the building was a monster, even compared to the other Mega-blocks which had become a common sight throughout the city. Each floor of the building was also taller than the average, adding extra stature to the obscenity of the tower of plexi-glass and reinforced steel.

A thick blanket of pollution created a considerable amount of cover over the city's streets, but not enough to prevent extreme nausea for any person unlucky enough to be suffering from vertigo.

A small crackle attacked Carly's eardrums as she powered up her amplified headphones with a single touch. The plectrum in her right hand flicked against the bottom two strings of her guitar, playing open notes in sequence, whilst the fingers on her left began to loosen in preparation to attack the neck of the seven-string guitar. Carly's left hand scaled the fret board as she picked out an arrangement of high notes at the highest speed possible to the talented musician. The titanium and gold composite cones in her headphones went into overdrive, deciphering every highly driven note wirelessly beamed from her guitar. Beneath the cover of her mask, her face went into spasm as she instinctively mimicked the musical notes being played at a volume only audible in her own mind. The frantic pace of her guitar playing was close to the speed of the world record breaking 'E. Pearl'… but where Carly was pinched in speed, she excelled in precision, her fingers picking out every intended note with ease. Her relentless fret work was almost robotic with its faultless mastery. The musician's left hand changed stance, forgoing notes in place of low tone chords, composing a blistering riff that kept the right hand moving at the same work rate.

Carly jammed for a relentless fifteen minutes, playing her own style of classical infused thrash metal, mixed with a synthesised tone, unusual to her chosen style.

She wore a small, uncomfortable face mask to aid her intake of oxygen at extreme altitudes. The mask sealed itself against her face, vacuumed into position - occasionally sucking a little too much of one's face into the cup, forcing the wearer's lips to purse unnaturally. The breathing apparatus would automatically adjust the user's oxygen levels and for the most part, it functioned effectively… if breathing was kept to a slow and steady rate.

Despite the altitude… being alone on the rooftop was bliss.

Wherever she went, wherever she travelled, her guitar went with her. It was always on standby, ready to be played with the skilled execution she always enjoyed.

An abrupt beep in her headphones reminded her it was time to get to work. She immediately ended her jam session and tidied the guitar away into the case. The body was shaped in the form of a lightning bolt, a vibrant neon green, finished with a white neck and carbon-black strings. The custom-built guitar was an impressive sight for any guitar enthusiast, but her attachment was not as strong as the love she felt for the one hanging in pride of place back in her apartment.

With it safely packed away, Carly carefully opened her briefcase. Inside: a telescopic tripod and her Kalcikay 950: a long-range, high-powered, sniper rifle, designed for use at extreme altitudes. The rifle had been disassembled into seven sections ready to be manually reconstructed, a task Carly perfected to a timed twenty-seven seconds. Once the chamber was primed, the musician swapped roles. She transformed into a patient hunter, a stalker of the skies, an assassin - laying on the deck, staring down the rifle scope, and lining up the target.

Patiently, she waited…

Through a cluttered maze of mega-blocks, spires and antennas, 4,764 yards from the Kalcikay's glistening muzzle: a mechanically powered door opened, giving access to the rooftop. John Sharrd stepped out onto the roof, momentarily blinded by the blazing sun. She watched him pace along the rooftop, blissfully unaware of the sights targeting the centre of his forehead.

Patiently, she waited…

A long, silver, crushed velvet dinner dress was uncommon attire for a sniper, but it didn't feel any less comfortable than the tactical gear she had spent years training in.

A spasm triggered on Carly's left cheek, just above the edge of her mask. The spasm was not from nerves, or from any kind of faltering concentration… it was simply one of those weird, unexplainable spasms which randomly occur and are completely uncontrollable.

Carly tapped her cheek with her fingertips, attempting to cease the spasm, but still it continued.

A small breeze caressed her face.

The slight chill was not nearly enough to cool her from the effect of the hot sun or even dull the niggling spasm.

She shrugged off the irritation and retuned her focus.

Two beads of sweat trickled down the back of her neck, weaving between the roots of her braids, before finding a path down the left-hand side of her ribcage… she failed to notice their presence.

The mask sealed over her nose and mouth began to slip as her skin softened in the sweltering heat… its function was unimpaired.

Despite the dizzying altitude, familiar sounds of city chaos flooded the air… yet every sound was now inaudible.

A fractional adjustment for wind shift. A quick review of the gun's stability. Carly was ready to take the shot. The hunter's nerves set in stone… determined to ignore every distraction. Her focus was fixed.

Carly watched as John Sharrd made his way to the edge of the helipad, his eyes watching the sky for his employer's approach. Methodically, she scanned the skyline through her scope.

She spotted the helicopter before John, and carefully tracked its journey to the roof.

Carly released her grip of the rifle and tied her braided locks into a tight ponytail, ensuring they kept clear of her face. She rolled her shoulders, cracking cartilage and bone, before positioning herself at the scope of the Kalcikay 950 once again.

She checked the time: 14:49 'right on schedule'.

The helicopter reached the rooftop and began its descent towards the landing marker.

Carly aimed, held her breath and squeezed the trigger, immediately ejecting the spent shell from the guns chamber. The large calibre bullet twisted through the thin city air before punching through the helicopter's side window and burrowing into the pilot's skull. The transport plummeted towards the helipad.

The sole passenger, Arnold Tames, opened his door and attempted to jump clear of the crash, but instead fell victim to his own transportation - diced into slivers of meat and bone by the rotor blades of the uncontrolled vehicle.

John Sharrd attempted to jump clear of the carnage headed towards him, but a second shot from the Kalcikay tunnelled through his head, mid-jump. His lifeless body slid across the concrete before being engulfed by flames from the downed transport. The fire raged across the rooftop - only twisted spires of metal poked out from the flickering glow of the blaze.

Carly adjusted the focus on her scope and waited attentively for forty-five seconds to confirm the kills…

Mission accomplished.

Dis-assembling the gun, she neatly packed it away into the briefcase, ready to make her stealthy retreat.

Before the assassin could straighten herself, she was knocked down to the floor.

Blood drenched her silver dress.

A crushing pain washed over her entire body.

Fumbling around in a wild frenzy, she kicked up clouds of dirt and dust. She desperately searched for a wound, but the panic had overwhelmed her and decimated any focus that once characterised the cool assassin and mastered musician. Carly knew she had been shot and she knew she was in grave danger, but she was incapable of finding a wound amongst the filthy, bloody mess covering her torso.

Desperate to scream, Carly rolled onto her back and slammed her fists into her chest. An explosion of blood and bile splattered the inside of her mask. She coughed and spluttered, frantically fighting for oxygen.

Claustrophobia weighed down on her as the bloodied mask clogged up and failed to assist her feed of oxygen.

She rubbed her face hysterically against her right shoulder, trying to release the small pressurised mask from its locked position on her cheeks.

She slammed her head backwards against the rooftop, reacting to the nauseating sensation of her sinuses flooding with the bloody cocktail of fluids rushing up through her throat.

The mask's seals ruptured under the wealth of fluids gathering around the edges of the small cup and the mask finally depressurised, allowing her to shake it from her face.

Carly slammed her fists into her chest once more...

A thick wad of blood and bile somersaulted into the air, before landing across the breadth of her face, covering her eyes and almost obscuring her vision.

She desperately fought against the agonising pain, battling with every pain receptor exploding inside her brain. The fight sapped every ounce of available energy from her body... yet the pain continued... and grew stronger with every passing second.

Inside her backpack was an emergency injector, crammed with enough chemicals to stimulate an adult elephant. She always carried the injector in case of emergency... however, her mind was unable to focus, the shock had set in and all her logical thoughts had been lost...all except for one...

There was only one person who knew she was on the rooftop of the Lifestyle News building: the man who hired her.

She screamed out in anger.

Tears streamed from her eyes but could not wash away the blood and spit beginning to glue her eyelids shut.

Her muscles seized before going numb.

She focused her remaining energy and gasped for breath, hungry for the sparse oxygen in the thin air.

The polluted sky turned black and Carly lost her fight with consciousness.

4

Seven years had passed since the assassination of Arnold Tames and John Sharrd. The killings had put an abrupt end to John Sharrd's investigation into the increasing pollution problems cursing the city. In the recent years, pollution levels had reached record highs, almost doubled since his research began. Human mutations were on the rise and the smog above the city's street became a major issue, sparking many violent riots. Government buildings suffered numerous attacks by angry mobs, putting severe stress on the city's police, who were over-worked and outnumbered more than ever before. The city's spiralling population growth only added to the relentless chaos.

Despite all the troubles amidst the general public and the threats of a civil revolution, one man stood at the top and clawed in healthy profits from the city's decline: Thomas Harthen, elected mayor three days after the murders of Arnold Tames, John Sharrd and one unnamed helicopter pilot. Harthen had his hands in every filthy pie available to him and showed no signs of stopping his reign of power and greed.

The confusion of waking up and not knowing where you are and how you got there is never a good start to the day.

Waking up with electrodes protruding from your body, tubes fed into your mouth and nose; surrounded by the drone of constantly bleating machines keeping you from death; your body numb, sapped of all its strength; your eyes burning from the blinding light as they try to adjust to being opened for the first time in many years; feeling overwhelmed by the sense of loneliness as the room you are in feels like a cramped prison cell... well, that must be a really bad start to the week.

Carly tried to sit up, but the lower part of her body was

unresponsive to any instructions given by her brain. The upper part of her body was weak and setting her pain receptors on fire… but everything from the waist down was just numb.

Frustrated, Carly slammed her fists into the bed repeatedly and tried to scream out for help, but no sound followed.

She slammed her fists into her chest and continued to stretch her vocal cords until finally, a scream balled out from her lungs.

Her cries were answered as the only door to the room burst open and two nurses hurried in.

'Miss, you must calm down before you do yourself any harm. Please, Miss?' one of the nurses pleaded as she reached out and firmly clutched Carly's flailing arms. On a normal day, Carly could have easily broken free from the nurse's grasp, and possibly snapped her forearm in two places, but she found she was far too weak to resist.

'Where am I? What the fuck is going on?' Carly sobbed as she gave up her fight with the nurse.

'You're in good hands, Miss!' reassured the second nurse as she held a warm, wet towel to Carly's head. 'You must relax, Miss!'

'Stop calling me Miss! Don't you know my name?'

'You came in as a Jane Doe, we have no record of who you are. You have been in a coma for seven years now, Miss.'

'Seven years, what the fuck? How am I still here? Why did you keep me plugged in? Surely after seven years... is this a fucking joke?'

'Miss, this is a privately funded clinic, it is not the same as a general hospital. Our employer, he wanted you to stay alive, we all tried very, very hard... he hoped… we all hoped you would pull through,' informed the first nurse. The bedside manner of the nurse was unusual, she kept smiling at Carly like a lunatic.

'Our employer will be along soon. Please, Miss, try to relax,' added the second nurse. 'We'll leave you in peace now. Come along, Sue.' She barked at her colleague as she began backing out of the room. The other nurse followed behind her, still wearing a large, uncomforting smile.

Carly reached out as they left the room, trying to grab the nurse's attention but the door had already closed behind them.

Seven years, what the fuck? Carly asked herself in disbelief. Something did not fit, and she knew it.

Why had she been kept alive for so long? It was unlikely she had been identified. As a security measure she had an almost invisible existence. As a Jane Doe, with no traceable family, it meant she should have been left to bow-out-quietly years ago. The machines would have been kept on for twelve months at the most. Who wanted to keep Carly alive? It made no sense. Someone wanted to see her wake up, but who and for what purpose?

Her troubled thoughts were interrupted by the arrival of a new visitor to her room: a tall, hulking man, with a receding hairline and a short, tatty ponytail just about long enough to tie back. Dressed in a grey business suit and dark green shirt of the finest quality, his attire showcased considerable wealth. He walked in smiling and rubbing his hands together firmly as if to warm them. Carly studied his face, his stature, his mannerisms, but he was unfamiliar to Carly, she had no memory of seeing him before.

'Carly, you must have many questions! I don't have the answers to them all, I am no doctor, so let's start with the basics, shall we?' The visitor stepped towards Carly with a confident rigidity, displaying his professional, business-like manner. 'You were left to die on that roof and to be honest... you probably should have. The gunshot to your back... unfortunately... well...' he hesitated, debating how to break the news 'it has paralysed you from the waist down. It was either a poor shot or the shooter wanted you to bleed to death, but with your extensive knowledge of human anatomy, Carly, I don't really need to be telling you this. You were found on the roof by chance, by some random maintenance worker, who - lucky for you - was caring enough to... Well, that is not important! Anyway... I intercepted you, I got you here and I have had a team of skilled professionals ensuring you had every available chance of recovery. I am very glad to see you have woken. On the road to recovery, this is a huge step!'

A storm raged inside Carly's head. The acceptance of taking a bullet when she was always very precise with her planning, always very watchful of her surroundings, always so calculated about where she chose to make a shot from, was impossible for her to comprehend. She thought about what her visitor had suggested, that the bullet was either a miss or a hit designed to cripple her and leave her to drain away. She knew the hit on her was meant to be an absolute. Whoever made the shot, had wanted her dead - *it would be a foolish risk to give her a chance of surviving.*

Only one man knew Carly was on that roof... 'Harthen! It was him, he had me fucking shot!'

'He didn't just have you shot... he took the shot himself, from over a mile out! He fancied himself as a freelance assassin, doing his own hits for his own gain. All those evenings down at his private range, he thought he had become a crack shot. I guess he was wrong?'

'Tying up loose ends?' asked Carly, already aware of the answer. 'Fucker! He should have confirmed the kill, a good start in the career of an assassin, eh?'

'What better way to tie up loose ends, than to eradicate them? You see, in the years you were gone, Thomas Harthen has become the most powerful man in the city, not only financially but politically. With the help from his powerful and particularly corrupt connections, Thomas has become Mayor of our fine city!'

'I wouldn't call this city 'fine'. Not unless things really have undergone a dramatic change in the last seven years?'

'A figure of speech, nothing more. In fact, times are worse than ever. Let's cut to it, shall we? I need you, Carly...' he placed a hand on his neck and wrenched his head to one side as he let out a quiet grunt, 'I need you to kill Thomas Harthen!'

He placed a hand on Carly's shoulder and locked himself into her gaze, attempting to gain trust.

'Are you mad? I can't even feel my legs, let alone walk. You've just told me this... this fucking situation, it isn't temporary, it's fucking permanent!" Carly's voice raised with her temper as she frantically processed the last ten minutes. 'Wait! I... I know you? I know your voice? You're *The Surgeon*, you used to be my contact, you used to arrange my targets, before...'

'Yes, that is correct. That was before Harthen took over, and I became his assistant.' The visitor slowly shuffled to the door and pulled the blinds shut. 'I am also the surgeon who operated on you, after you were shot, I got you out of the shit and my team nursed you ...kept you alive. Harthen, he made the typical rookie mistake of writing down the address of where you would shoot John Sharrd from... and I intercepted that information when I was at his home, umm... *collecting...* rather, erm... sensitive documents. These documents were meant to help put a stop to his increasing growth of power. I had hoped to get to Harthen before he got to you, but alas, I was too late. For that, my dear, I am truly sorry.'

'You have already lied to me. You said you are no doctor, but that isn't true... maybe Harthen wasn't the only person aware of the hit on Sharrd? How can I trust anything you say?' Carly twisted and contorted as she struggled in her bed, attempting to get up, but her efforts were futile. 'I always assumed your name was just a code name you had picked up, but I see it's not really a code name, is it? I am grateful to you for keeping me alive, but I cannot go back to the life I had, I can't even fucking stand. I would have been better off dead! Surely you must have someone else you can call now, why the fuck ask me?'

'I like you Carly, I like your efficiency, I like how damn good you are at what you do. Out of all the jobs I have thrown your way, you have never failed. Three hits I have put on Harthen so far, but his wealth and his power have prevailed and now I have been driven to exile. I have been under permanent lock-down for two years, hiding from the growing price now sitting on my own head... ironic really. I need to scrub the world clean of Thomas Harthen, his reign needs to end... and to be perfectly frank, I need my life back!' The Surgeon paced the room, clenching his fists, and spitting as he talked, there was clearly some truth in his story, *but how much*? was a question that remained unanswered.

'I want to get this fucker, more than you do, believe me! I have a taste of vengeance in my mouth, a stain of hatred imprinted on my damn mind. I know he was a keen rifleman. I know his ego is gargantuan, the daft fucker couldn't even remain as an anonymous contact whilst commissioning hits. He had to show his ugly face... show he was the one in charge. Believe me, I want him gone... but this thirst you have for vengeance... it has clearly deluded you...' Carly ripped the bedsheets from her body and slapped her own legs furiously. 'I can't use these anymore, I am as good as dead myself.' She sniffled, breaking into a flood of tears.

The Surgeon calmly collected two glasses from a row of cupboards hanging on the far wall of the room. He poured a large measure of whisky in each before downing one and handing the other to Carly. Keeping whisky in the cupboard of a recovery room seemed like an unusual thing to do, but nothing about Carly's situation was likely to have been written in any textbook of what was considered 'usual'. It wasn't her preferred beverage, but her mouth was dry, and her brain was working overtime and needed to be numbed. The whisky worked its way down her throat like volcanic lava carving a new path down a mountain side. The potent volume of alcohol in the small glass of straight-whisky was not the most thirst-quenching refreshment that could have passed Carly's lips after a long, seven-year stint in med-bay... but there was no hesitation in knocking it back.

'What if I told you that you can have your shot at revenge? What if I told you that I can give that to you? What if I gave you a way to fight, a way to be yourself again?' The Surgeon collected Carly's empty glass and returned to the whisky bottle for a top up. It was a fine, single malt, aged to perfection, wearing an expensive label - *he may well have been in hiding from Thomas Harthen, but he certainly had a good stock of supplies*. He handed Carly the fresh whisky and gently perched on the edge of her bed, raising his glass as if to toast. 'What if I told you I can give you new, improved, more powerful legs, and then...'

The Surgeon sprung from the edge of the bed in a theatrical, almost camp, fashion and walked over to a large cupboard door in the corner of the room. A dramatic pause and a cheeky wink in her direction caused Carly to hesitate before knocking back the second serving of whisky.

The Surgeon slowly opened the door to reveal an unmistakable object: Carly's briefcase... the case which housed her Kalcikay rifle. It stood on end, leaning against a second, even more distinctive case... the case of her cherished neon-green travel guitar.

'Carly, I can give you new and improved legs. Then you leave here, taking your belongings... and then... then you may have your revenge!'

SEVEN STRING KILLER
BY **TANIA TAYLOR**

Angry Itch

1

All the self-obsessed, fame hungry, attention seeking wannabees.

All the surgically enhanced, the digitally corrected, image-fixated ghosts out there - looking for constant approval.

All the pierced, body-modified, face-painted clowns with their sprawling body ink on display - hoping to be noticed as individuals.

All the self-made 'stars' scratching around for a piece of notoriety, in turn throwing away any scrap of self-respect, any morsel of dignity, putting themselves on wafer-thin pedestals for a world of maggots with a five-second attention span.

All the wasters who refuse to earn a living - the spongers, the scroungers, the bottom-feeders, the parasites, the ones who rely on the taxes paid up by the hard-working people of the world to keep the lazy in a state of unwarranted luxury.

All the drones who believe their own lives offer more importance, more significance, more value than that of the next person...

What makes you so special?

Why do your words of knowledge and wisdom need to be heard?

Who do you think you are?

All the suits, the politicians, the real-estate traders, the bankers, the corrupt men and women behind your giant corporate desks, stowed away in your lavish, fully furnished offices, sitting there, smiling your heads off in your huge towers of steel and concrete, watching over the city as you bleed it dry…

You disgust me.

You all fucking disgust me.

You make me sick to the core.

I AM COMING FOR YOU ALL!

2

I sit here… and I wait.

I wait for the world to burn... but it just seems to keep on ticking... it keeps on thriving...

Like a fucking cancer!

Injustice seems to be commonplace - the innocent and the needy, they suffer, and they call out.

They call out their blood-curling screams. Screams that may as well be silent whispers, for no one listens... no one cares.

People don't care... the human race has become a collective of parasites. Perhaps they have always been fucking parasites? I wish for them all to be eradicated.

I cannot stand the smell of this place anymore. It has become infested with humans - you can barely move throughout the day without coming in to contact with their infestation. People scurry around, bumping into one another. They offer no apologies for nearly knocking each other to the ground - not to the young, to the old, to the weak, to the disadvantaged. They are all in such a bloody hurry to get where *they* are going, their only thoughts are for themselves. They scurry around and they don't even make eye contact with one another! What the fuck have we become?

I remember the time, long ago, before this place was even a city - it was just a small town, a kind, friendly town. Then the powerful, greedy, selfish, big-money corporations moved in and started throwing around their riches, sucking all the energy and all the hope from the rest of us. First: homes were thrown together in their thousands - mainly houses and small apartment buildings, but then... the houses were taken away, demolished, faster than they were being thrown up, skyscrapers became commonplace. Next: gigantic towers sprung up, monstrosities which dwarfed everything else in their shadow - the government called them 'Mega-blocks'… as if the skyscrapers littering the skyline weren't obscene enough. When the first mega-block was built, that was when the mayor called this fucking hole a 'City'. I don't really know the politics of it all, hell, I don't even care... it's all wrong if you ask me! How can so many people be crammed into one building? Living on top of each other in their thousands? They breathe each other's air, sucking in the germs, the filth... It doesn't matter how advanced your air-conditioning systems are, when you are crammed in that damn tight, you will still consume human waste... and there is plenty of that in this city.

You would have thought once people witnessed the first *block war* - when neighbouring families slaughtered each other on their doorsteps for seemingly trivial fucking reasons - that would be the time when someone in charge would have stepped up and said: *'Fuck! This is bad... this is chaos!'* It doesn't look like anyone ever did though... and if they did, no fucker ever listened.

At night, in the shroud of darkness, you don't need military-grade thermal imaging to see the despair on the streets, it is almost impossible not to see it...

We are all inert witnesses to the horrors in the shrouds of the darkness.

I can't bear to think of what this place has become It sickens me to the very depths of my bowels. A pungent taste of disgust lays in my mouth, clinging to every moist surface... it is always there, I can't ever wash it away.

I believe that I used to be a happy man.

I believe I was once a carefree man...

...but honestly...

I wouldn't like to say for sure. I could have fucking imagined it...

This crazy world has eaten away at my damn mind. Reality seems to be as much of a stranger to me as the woman who just walked past the window.

Through my disgust... my hatred... my anger, I have concluded that I must do something about this world. I must make a stand against the people in power who profit from the misery of those beneath them.

These bombs will be the answer!

Once these things go off, that bastard mayor will be gone. That fucker: Billy Banstead. How he ever came to power, I do not understand. Corruption? Of course, corruption! Corruption is always the answer. Billy Banstead is the biggest meat farmer in the world, when all us mere mortals can lay our hands on is tasteless, synthetic crap - the rich get to enjoy the real food. I can't remember the last time I ate real meat. I'm not sure if I will ever have the privilege again. I long for its taste. I long for it to pass through my lips. To be chewed, savoured, enjoyed... devoured once again.

The city's feeble excuse for a police force... they will soon see what being *undermanned* and *overstretched* really is. They will wish they had made more economical use of their big cash injections from their numerous, hefty bribes... We all know it goes on, everyone fucking knows... but nobody has the power or the guts to put an end to it.

The gangs who have a tight grip on the city, who force us to comply, scare us into turning blind eyes to their brutal, vicious ways... I will watch them suffer for their crimes. I will bring down their empires, and they will all burn too!

The trigger system on this thing is something I am especially proud of. There's no chance of being caught by the blast, I could trigger it from the other side of the world if I so wished...

...but then I wouldn't be able to see the fireworks...

...I wouldn't be able to watch the carnage.

Here on the streets, I can watch the fucking rats scurry around in their pathetic, pointless panic as my bombs go boom, boom, boom... all over the city.

The fallout is going to be something that will be remembered for a century... heck, maybe until the end of fucking time?

After they're triggered, things will never be the same. This forsaken city will have no choice but to change. People will have to band together... I will become the saviour of the people.

There will be a new beginning.

There will be a new dawn.

This quaint little diner has always been a frequent visit of mine. It has always had pretty shitty staff, with the pitiful look of defeat and misery slapped all over their faces. At least the food they serve me is good. Not that I have explored the menu extensively, I order the same thing every time I come here: tofu and synthi-eggs. It tastes great and the portions are as generous as those served up by my grandmother every Sunday afternoon. Coming here is, in many ways, the highlight of my week... pathetic, isn't it? The aptly named 'Greasy Sam's Diner', is about as exciting as life gets for people like me. No wonder the staff here look like they have won the lottery but lost the ticket.

This grubby, yet quaint little diner is going to be demolished in two days, levelled, making room for a giant cruise liner to be constructed, right in the heart of the fucking city, of all places. The ship won't ever see the water, despite it being only 10 miles or so from the damn sea. It will just sit there, cast into the concrete, an eye-sore, surrounded by the glass and steel of the mega-blocks.

There is a big fuss over this thing, you can't escape the constant nattering about it. Designed to cater for those with deep pockets. The sort of pockets that would deem the monthly wage of your regular Joe, loose change. *Fuck*, the divide between rich and poor, it makes me sick!

The Yachtsman Plaza, they're going to call it... sounds like a damn pantomime dance!

Catching a glimpse of myself in the mirror on the wall, just about recognisable behind the clutter of the colourful, heavy branding of *'the world's number one soft-drink'*, I make out the image of a man who has been a victim of this city and its ways.

I squeeze my eyes shut and I dream...

The short, neatly trimmed hair. The dark blue suit with designer labels sewn into the collar. The combination coded, snake-skin suitcase, complete with a toughened, platinum security chain. The diamond encrusted gold watch with precision engineered movements. The antique leather shoes, spotlessly polished to a finish to reflect your face back at you every time you gaze into them... These were not the things I would ever see from the man in the mirror. My life isn't going to turn out that way, no matter how much I dream.

I open my eyes and I gaze into the mirror… the reality is daunting. I sit here sporting a buzz-cut that attempts to mask the ever-growing widow's peak. A scruffy black beard with far too many wispy, grey hairs. A pair of black jeans hanging from my almost starved, medically unhealthy frame. A loose t-shirt which used to be a brilliant white but is now beginning to resemble a used dish cloth. A watch I purchased from a market stall across the street: if I am lucky it tells the right time at least twice a day. A wallet in my right-hand pocket held together with industrial tape - its contents barely enough to pay for this cup of cheap tea I am struggling to drink, let alone front the cost of the delicious meal I eagerly await. A pair of imitation leather boots which have become so cracked and battered, they look more dishevelled-grey than deep-black… Life has not quite worked out like my dreams.

The market outside the diner is one of the only parts of this city that reminds me of the old times, the old ways of life when people used to talk to each other in the street. Out in the market there is conversation, bargaining, banter, friendly smiles, and audible laughter… but walk past the market and everyone becomes a stranger to one another, nobody would dare to even make eye contact with a passer-by. Even this diner has become a part of the city and the ways of the damned. Apart from the shitty waitress who served me with my tea, nobody in here has made eye contact with me. Not that I search to acknowledge their existence either… there's no point, they're all fucking doomed anyway.

3

Fifteen-minutes have passed since I ordered my damn food. I'm starting to get a bit cranky. The waitress should have known my order as soon I had walked through the door... it's the same as I always have: flavoured tofu and synthi-eggs...

...what the fuck is taking that bloody kitchen so long?

Every time I come here, I practice spinning a knife around my hand, swapping it between my fingers, trying to perfect a smooth motion... one day I will crack it, one day it'll look *polished and cool*, like a scene from a martial arts movie or something.

What the fuck is taking so long, where is my food?

The hunger in my belly is begging me to complain, but that's not my style. I jab the handle of the knife into my gut, trying to silence the gargling.

I see so many people complain about trivial things, things that just don't matter. The other day there was a guy in here, he called over the waitress and complained his coffee had too much milk... a fair point usually, perhaps? Something that would normally warrant catching the attention of the busy staff and make a polite request for a new drink? *But this fucker...* this fucker had poured the damn milk in the coffee himself! How the fuck can one complain and then demand a fresh cup, when he was the stupid asshole who ruined it in the first place? I sat here, in this very fucking seat, and I watched as the man made the young waitress withdraw into a shell, petrified of his escalating temper and complete over-reaction to his own stupid fucking error. People complain about such trivial things... it makes me sick! I wanted to get up and stab him in the throat with the knife that I was spinning in my hand that day. I wanted to stand over him and watch him bleed out, waiting for the worried panic on his face to morph into realisation that his demise was his own doing, his own stupid mistake - that would have taught him a fucking lesson... but I am not one to create a scene. So, I just sat here in this very seat and waited patiently. Eventually the guy stormed out. He shortly returned to throw a brick at the door: it didn't even break the strengthened glass. There wasn't even a scratch. *What a fucking moron!*

A child sits across the diner from me now, I realise he has been fixated on me for the last few minutes... I have no idea why, but I'm finding him increasingly disturbing. I am not used to the eye contact, not even in here. Alarm bells in my head tell me I should ignore him and get moving, trigger these bombs, and get the fuck out of town... but the child's stare has driven me into an uncomfortable state of paralysis that keeps feeding my curiosity: *Why is this child looking at me? What have I done to draw his attention so intensely? Does he know what I intend to do - what I need to do?*

The air conditioning in here has never been great, but today it seems to be spitting out waves of sticky grease and rancid sweat, leaving a funky taste in my mouth... *or am I just imagining it? Maybe it is this child making me feel uneasy... guilty?*

My throat seems to dry out completely and an involuntary ticking has started at the back of my mouth, irritating the roof. I try to imagine what kind of weird spasms are causing the annoying ticking... my unprofessional diagnosis is blaming my saliva glands, it's as if they are trying to kick start themselves and force moisture back into my throat...I'm no doctor, I have no idea what is going on inside there, but it is almost audible now.

I hack up phlegm into my throat as quietly as possible, trying not to draw attention to my bizarre irritation… it doesn't work, it just carries on fucking ticking.

I close my eyes and try to relax.

I breathe slowly through my nose.

I try… I try to relax

The ticking soon fades - either I learn to ignore it, or it just disappears... I wish the rest of life was as easy to battle.

The uneasy feeling that the bemused child has put upon me soon passes also, once the waitress finally brings me my meal.

The eggs look pale and inedible, the same as they always do, but they taste fucking great. The tofu also resembles nothing that I would care to put in my mouth, but it too tastes bloody good. This is not a meal to be devoured with your eyes. The waitress chuckles at me as I finish tasting the food before she has even placed it down in front of me. A passing comment about my lack of patience is enough to make the left-hand side of my mouth break into an awkward smile... she winks at me and walks away. I have seen this waitress a hundred times before, and she always seems to look slightly different. It's hard to imagine that someone could create so many different hair styles with that mass of hair. Today she has kept up the tradition of change: at first glance, her blue and red hair is bundled into a ponytail, but it's not just any ponytail, she has jammed two silver rods through it. They stick out at the top and run down past her shoulders, her hair twisting and wrapping around them in a strange and intricate zigzag fashion. The look is quite beautiful, but oddly irritating at the same time. It's easy to imagine that the two rods running down her neck are restricting her head movements, although I am yet to see evidence of any issues incurred by the funky hairstyle.

I have never understood fashion. I find it very difficult to comprehend why anyone would want to draw attention to themselves. It's certainly something I have no desire to do - especially not today.

Watching people trying to follow trends. Watching them attempt to create their own fashions. All in the naivety that they are individuals in a world of millions-upon-millions, stacked on top of each other. They exist in a population far too rampant to comprehend the numbers. The need to be one of the sheep... it just makes me sick!

How can these people go through their days with such a deluded evaluation of self-worth?

It is time...

Time to get things moving.

Time to make people re-evaluate their lives and their pitiful existence.

Time to show this city that it cannot continue to be a breeding ground for filth.

I have my trigger. Home made from an old rocker switch that used to activate the fuel pump in my father's archaic sports car. Damn, he loved that thing... until it became his demise when he tried to mate it with a great-big fucking tree, *poor guy.* The switch is now mounted on a metal box. It houses the intricate circuitry and workings to transmit a trigger signal to the multiple explosives I have placed in key positions around this city. I have spent many hours finding the right positioning for each bomb... ensuring that every blast counts... for maximum effect.

As soon as I step outside this diner, that's it... I'm flicking the switch.

I throw down enough money to pay the bill and leave a tip for the waitress... *even though my food took forever to arrive.*

As I head out the door, the child across the diner catches my attention again. The little fucker isn't doing anything, he is just leaning over the back of his chair, staring into me, his eyes boring into my soul. His parents don't seem to be paying him any attention at all. They don't even seem to be paying attention to each other. The non-communicative couple just keep shovelling food into their lazy mouths as they tap away on their personal communication devices.

I'm about to leave and he's still fucking staring at me, watching me obsessively as I move towards the door.

Then something else happens... something unexpected... something truly unnerving...

...He smiles at me...

...*the little fucker*...

... he actually fucking smiles at me!

The pure, untainted, childish innocence in his smile strikes me like a fucking thunderbolt to the heart.

In a single moment... with one single, collaborative movement of the tiny muscles in the face of this small, innocent stranger... my world crumbles.

My house of bricks and steel caves in on me as if it were made of mud and wet tissue paper.

Everything I had been telling myself... preaching to myself to justify my plans - all the hatred for people, all the anger for this world and the wretched stench of this city...

It just crumbles!

The child, he looks right into me, he sees something I thought was lost a long time ago...

Humanity.

His stare was uneasy...

...but his smile is

...it's cleansing?

I feel free from the anger boiling inside of me.

He turns and faces his table as the waitress brings him a chilled desert of sugary delights. His fixation with me is lost when better, finer things capture his attention - better things than this washed up, bitter old-man.

I hear him giggle.

I smile... I can't help it... I actually fucking smile.

I clutch the door handle and tug at it - the door always seems to stick. It needs attention, like the rest of this building.

As the door opens, I feel like it is the doorway into my mind. I feel like I am releasing all my negativity into the sweltering hot, city air. I feel like perhaps... I will go on to do good things.

I feel great!

I feel a release.

My right foot crosses the boundary between the diner and the heavily littered street...

I pause...

I turn to look at the child once more and I smile at the carefree innocence.

I smile at the joy in the sugary dessert.

I smile at the beauty of the human spirit.

I smile at hope...

I smile at the future.

The trigger in my hand now feels exhaustingly heavy. I can feel it weighing on my shoulder like a sack of large rocks, hanging from my fingertips.

My conscience climbs into the heavy sack and increases the weight tenfold, I can feel it tugging at my arm, begging me not to use the trigger.

I look at the device in my hand…

It is brilliantly engineered and constructed.

A small, red-light flashes…

It tells me it is primed and ready.

My mind floods with imaginary photographs. They flutter around in a cyclone of confusion and then stop. They float around in the dead space of my mind. They become weightless… slowly cascading to the dark, empty floor of my brain.

I focus hard on the photographs, trying to decipher the blurred images.

I shrug my shoulders and shake my head frantically.

Every picture becomes clear.

Each one is a vivid image of my homemade bombs, sitting in wait throughout the city.

They lay discreetly, patiently… just waiting for me to flick the switch and make them sing.

I swing the door back and forth with my hand, lost in a moment of emptiness.

The hinges squeak, almost silently. I question whether anyone else can hear them as I attempt to create a rhythm with the irritating noise.

I close my eyes, draw in a deep breath and as I exhale, I push the door shut firmly.

I turn…

I walk over to the child at the table and kneel beside him.

His father drags his attention from his empty plate he seemed to be transfixed with and looks at me with a curious, baffled look on his face... I ignore him.

The child's mother is oblivious to my presence, lost in her ignorance… deep in her solitary, digital world.

I draw the child's attention by gently prodding him on his left shoulder. He looks at me blissfully and I ask him if he wants something to play with…

He eagerly accepts, the look on his face is sheer joy and childish excitement, the type that I had long forgotten.

I attempt to mimic the smile he showed me earlier... I look

like a goon and I know it.

I stand up straight, stretching my back gently before relaxing my shoulders and releasing a lung full of air.

I place the box on the table next to his dessert.

He becomes fascinated by the beautiful glow of the blinking red light.

I nod at the child, and then ruffle my hands through his hair in an awkward, uncomfortable sign of affection.

I wink playfully at the child's confused father, then make my way to the exit.

As I open the diner door once again, I hear the squeak... nobody else seems to notice it.

I pause... my hand holds the door stationary... the squeaking stops...

I turn back and call out to the carefree, innocent child...

'There ya go kid... Have fun with that!'

ANGRY ITCH
BY **BARBARA BALE**

John Grand

John Grand

The angels came to me that night.

The angels came and they plucked me from the murky bowels of despair.

I was alone. I was beaten down. I was battered, bruised and torn apart. I was inches from being in a much darker hole than the one where I all too frequently dwell. A dark, rancid hole from which there would have been no return... but the angels came and they saved me.

I was in danger of losing my wretched soul to the unrepentant, hungry beasts that feast on the carcasses of the weak... they waited.

They waited for me to give my weakened body over to them so they could consume the marrow in my bones.

They waited for my mind to break so they could thrive on any essence of life that still lay dormant in the hidden corridors of my being.

The angels came to me that night...

The angels came to me and gave me a chance for one... last... fucking hurrah.

I knew what I had to do. I knew I had to be fast, merciless and unforgiving. I knew it was going to get loud.

The shoulder holsters gripped my twin-boys tight to my beating chest. The Boys were cocked and loaded, ready to go. That wasn't unusual, the Boys were always ready to go, always ready to get loud. They loved to bark and shout in the thunderous glory of the kill.

I picked myself up from the stinking, muddy pool of blood, spit and rainwater that swelled beneath me on the dock. I could feel my muscles begging me to lay back down and rest, telling me to go to sleep, perhaps for the rest of my days. My bones told me the same story as they creaked and grumbled in a fading despair. There was no time to feel pain, no time at all. There was work to be done… and I sure as hell couldn't see anyone else getting this shit finished. It was down to me... me and the Boys.

The sodden clothes I had been wearing since early that morning clung to my aching body as I stretched, reached for the heavens and allowed the rage in my belly to cry out a glorious war cry. My hands clawed at the sky for a few seconds, searching for a God above to squeeze by the throat and question…

'Why me?'

I already knew the answer, but I wasn't ready to hear it. I abandoned my search for the infinite-being and grabbed my over-coat from the filthy waters beneath the dock - it used to be a fine coat, now it was just as battered, bruised and torn apart as I was... *perhaps it was no longer fit to be a coat?*

... damn shame!

I needed to get to where I was going fast and having the Boys on show could draw the sort of attention that would slow my stride, so the battered coat would have to suffice.

It was saturated and rank. The ice-cold water from the heavens poured off my body like a river that had burst its banks... I wasn't going to dry off any time soon - but being a little wet was the least of my worries.

I made my way to my bike...

She sat strong and proud under the streetlamp - exactly where I had left her. Her deep, black paintwork was iridescent - complimenting every glimpse of electrical light. The intricate chrome of her mechanical heart reflected an array of rainbows, playing carelessly in the darkness. The bike's chromium framework also gleamed and sparkled, catching every spectrum of moon and streetlight available. She was a thing of unnatural beauty.

I straddled her like a young cowboy straddling an eager stallion... she really was a sight to behold.

I knew the angels would look after her for me… I knew they would not see her harmed.

I kicked her into action. She growled in a joyous anger and she yelped… barking hysterically at the city night as I teased her delicate throttle.

Firing up all cylinders - she purred like a wild, untamed cat. Now... she too was ready to get to work.

For long seconds I examined her beauty...

Shimmering reflections across her chrome frame mirrored the swelling sea making her look as if she was quivering in pure excitement.

I ran my fingers across her bulging tank and gave her a warm pat of admiration.

Another tickle of the throttle and she cried out again.

I cast my left hand over the leather holster strapped below my saddle...

Then it hit me...

...something was different...

Before I had been left for dead, left to bleed out... face down in the murky pools of waste on the dock... the Boys shared their existence - they had company... *Martha!*

Martha was missing... gone from the holster strapped to the side of my bike!

What son of a bitch would take Martha from me? The bastards!

Another mark added to the list - another reason to kill.

The bike roared down the road as I opened the throttle, all its rage throbbing anxiously through the rear wheel, fighting in desperation to gain some grip and keep me in a straight line.

The god damned rain didn't stop!

I was hoping the high-speed ride would dry me off, but the skies continued to weep. Maybe the big man upstairs knew what I was about to do? Perhaps he knew about the shit storm the Boys and I were ready to unleash? There was rage in my belly and no God could stop me, all he could do was empty the heavens and try to slow me down.

As my wheels thrashed through the waves trying to find their escape route from the city's streets, I noticed that the usual fight was unfolding outside Grace's strip joint. I didn't have time to stop and pick a side, there was other work to be done - these morons would have to sort it out for themselves. I pulled the throttle right back, pinning it against the stop - the engine roared and the front wheel leapt towards the darkness of the night sky. I could feel the increased anger spill out of my rear tyre… I knew the bike felt my pain.

I continued with my journey.

My bike, she knew...

…things were about to get loud!

I neared the warehouse - the two jacked-up, muscle-bound freaks standing guard outside the front weren't the sort of guys that I could easy tangle with, not in my physical condition.

The other bastards were undoubtedly cowering behind the doors… the ones who had tried to put me down… they failed, but they had seen to it that I wasn't up to my best. The usual stealthy, professional, calm approach… that was going to be a problem at this point.

I kept the bike pointed straight at the door behind the two guards.

I stood on the saddle, whipped the Boys from their holsters and fired two angry shots from each. One shot for each chest and another for each forehead.

Sprays of glorious blood painted the air.

I leapt from the bike like an acrobat as the guards collapsed to the ground: two down!

The bike smashed its way through the heavy security door, and I followed it.

Landing in a forward roll, I executed two more fuckers with perfect reactionary headshots… before I even got to my feet. The landing hurt like hell, and my bike was whimpering under a pile of rubble. There was undoubtedly damage inflicted to both myself and my bike, but there wasn't any time to check our wounds...

I would have to come back for her later.

A smug, wicked sense of amusement warmed me as I noticed the surprised look of a tiny little man who had witnessed my flight through the front door - he must have been impressed by my entrance. Unluckily for him, his machine gun denied his pleas to unload its clip and put me down early.

The puny fucker ran at me, hoping to take me down with force. A boot to the chest ended those dreams. My size nine sent him backwards through a thin plasterboard wall, which exploded on impact. It was pure luck that I managed to snatch his gun away from him... as my boot smashed into his ribcage.

Five down!

A sixth man came at me, waving around a giant blade that looked too heavy for his awkward hands. With my right hand holding both my pistol and my newly acquired machine gun, this sucker had to go down with just the gun in my left.

The lone Boy spat out two rounds - one through the cheek and the second, right between the eyes.

That god-damned sword of his flew out of his hands and nearly cut me in half. *Lucky I'm fast, or that could have been messy.*

I checked over the sword wielding scum: he was now in need of some serious surgery to repair what I had done to his pretty face. The first round had taken out the whole left cheek, teeth, gums - the lot... *maybe even a chunk of tongue if I wasn't mistaken?*

... hard to tell.

The second had given him a nose job that certainly fixed any sinus issues he may have had.

No doubt about it... he was a dead man for sure.

Maggot!

With the Boys holstered I checked over the machine-gun that had previously failed to unload into my chest. The tiny man had left the safety on... *Fool! I thought that shit only happened in the movies?*

A quick click of the toggle switch and the gun was live... I was ready to do some real killing!

I climbed through the hole in the plasterboard wall, entering an empty corridor. I trampled over the body of guy number five... but not before ramming the butt of his old machine gun into his rosy red lips a few times - just to be sure he wasn't going to get back up for another attempt on my life.

At the end of the corridor, a closed door sealed the tight space - that was my next destination. Behind that door, the corridor would open into an old inoperative warehouse. It had been out of use for many years, but now served as a hangout for thugs and scum. The room was alive with panicked fools, armed to the teeth and waiting to spill my blood.

There was no time to come up with an elaborate plan... I knew that as soon as I popped my ugly head out of the corridor, a hail of bullets would pummel me until I was drained of scarlet fluid - ending my fated mission of revenge.

Asshole number five…

…he had the solution.

Considering he was only a small man… he was a fucking dead weight. The blood and shit in his skull leaked out all over me as I held up his limp body… *Perhaps it wasn't the best idea to cave his face in with the butt of his own gun after all?*

The stench seeping from his wound was enough to make me urge… *And I'm no soft stomach, pansy-ass!*

I dragged his stinking corpse to the end of the corridor and retrieved four pins from the hand grenades strapped to his tactical vest.

I blew him a playful kiss before launching him into the closed door, busting it open with what remained of his skull. A flurry of bullets met his airborne, lifeless body, turning him into a mush of bloody flesh and bone.

I allowed myself a conceited grin as I tossed the four safety pins into the large room.

A chorus of screams sang out as the grenades detonated - my grin widened to a crazed smile.

The body of asshole five had decorated the main room of the warehouse. Body parts and internals showered the small army. Blood and guts flowing like a fucking horror movie.

With the satisfyingly gory distraction in place, I exited the corridor and stepped into the expanse of the warehouse. I immediately began picking off the bewildered mercenaries with precision shots from the machine gun. High speed bullets ended lives in an instant…

…*They shouldn't have fucked with me!*

The gun's magazine soon depleted, and the Boys were required to come out of their holsters and join in with the glory of the kill. For me… killing was always easy.

One big ugly mother fucker came at me with a knife. He

fought gallantly. At one point it looked like he was going to run his blade into my gut, but I jammed my right knee into his groin, and he buckled. I wrestled with him before thrusting his own blade up into his neck. The big guy's lower jaw dropped, and I was nearly blinded by the light reflecting off the blade in his mouth. I tightened my grip on the weapon and twisted it, searching for a route to his brain with the knife's sharp tip. His murky, hazel-brown eyes went cold. I released my grip on the knife and allowed him to drop to the floor in a heap.

I charged through the open room, picking up pace and racking up the body count - the small army of fools falling at my feet.

I took a few unlucky shots myself along the way - one in the left thigh, nearly stopping my stride. One grazed my right forearm... and a real lucky son-of-a-bitch took the top of my right ear clean off. A flurry of bullets zinged around the place as the battle raged and the Boys emptied their clips. I made the lucky son-of-a-bitch that shot my ear really suffer... I dislocated his jaw with the butt of the pistol in my right hand, then took out both of his kneecaps with the butt in my left. Once he was incapacitated, I gouged his fucking eyes out with my thumbs.

I left the poor sap on the floor to bleed out, it's what he deserved... I just wish he hadn't screamed like a fucking banshee as I took out his eyes... thanks to him, my ear was already giving me enough issues... his wailing only made it worse.

The blind man continued to cry out in pain until his last breath...

... *Noisy fucker!*

Fifteen fools down.

It's good to keep a tally, it adds to the sense of personal glory. Killing had always been something I was good at, a gift I was born with perhaps?

For me killing was as easy as breathing.

A small, metal stairwell led to an office on a gantry at the back end of the warehouse. I knew that inside the office, the biggest asshole waited: the man who gave the order to leave me for dead on the docks.

I holstered the Boys - still smoking from all the barking they had done, then collected the two sub-machine guns from a couple of dead bums laying on the warehouse floor.

My nerve centre was suddenly alive and sending bolts of pain through my body as I slowed and reached the stairwell.

'No time to slow down now.' I coughed, spitting out a wad of my own blood into the ugly, tortured face of one of the deceased gunmen.

My mind was full of rage... full of anger.

I fixed my attention to the door at the top of the stairs...

'...I'm coming..'.

...I am fucking coming for you!'

Breathing became a chore as I neared the top step... I stood still... waited to get my head together and gather my fading breath.

A filthy layer of thick blood painted the window of the office door. I attempted to wipe it clean, but the claret just gathered dust and smeared all over the glass.

I leaned my head against the window and peered into the office, through the haze of blood...

'Martha!'

The bastard had my shotgun, and was pointing it right at me, waiting for me to open the door and attempt to take him on.

The crazed smile on his face made the hairs on my neck stand to attention.

My clothes still clung to me - uncomfortable and restrictive, still soaked from the rain.

My nerve centre ceased from sending the signals of pain through my body, and instead fuelled me with a fierce fire that roared intensely.

The rage in my belly let out another war cry, louder and deeper than any I had mustered before.

I kept my attention on him, I stared into his eyes, peering into his soul.

He kept still. He was calm, focused, still smiling at me - *Fucker!*

No one takes Martha from me.
No one leaves me battered and bruised, left for dead!
No one takes Martha and then aims her straight at me!

It was time! Time for Martha and the Boys to be reunited.
No one takes Martha from me… not even my own brother!
He kept smiling at me…

…Things were about to get loud.

JOHN GRAND
BY TANIA TAYLOR

Secrets of Sanity

In shrouds of darkness the demons they hide,

From the world of chaos, the world that's outside.

Fragile minds they yearn to corrupt,

But a wicked mind, that's a mind to instruct.

A dormant spark they'll try to ignite,

But a cruel intent, is their intent to excite.

Tortured souls will search for their confession,

But it's an example for all, an example and lesson.

You may try to run and you may try to hide,

But the demons they come, they come…

from the inside.

Colin A May 2019

1

Living with insanity is never easy... Ian should know, he believes he has a higher calling from the demons who speak to him every day.

The demons have a visual presence, but only in Ian's mind... to everyone else these demons were simply the excuse that Ian used to carry out his ultra-violent outbursts. Leeza however - she knew the demons were imaginary, she also knew Ian was insane... she was just happy to be along for the ride.

Ian had taken a contract from George Stern - the fierce leader of a criminal organisation currently rising through the ranks of the city's underworld. The contract would utilise Ian Roster's specialist set of skills: Destruction, Bloodshed and Chaos. George Stern had never shared with Ian why he wanted the computer room of Deacon Plastics destroyed, nor did Ian care to ask, Stern just offered him a sum of money and told him: 'This is the right thing to do'...

That was all Ian's demons needed to hear.

Ian had previously served as a seek and destroy agent under an unofficial government contract until he was discharged for severe mental instability. No longer an asset to the government, and an increasing threat to their illegal, unsanctioned operations, a hefty price was placed on his head. Leeza Greene, a working-girl and part-time assassin took the contract.

She had been given instructions to meet with Ian's only known associate, obtain Ian's location, and terminate him... an easy task for someone with Leeza Greene's skillset.

The first part of her task was routine: Ian's associate was easy to manipulate, easily seduced by her charm and looks... generous servings of alcohol also helped her cause. After a few hours of talking, drinking and fucking, Ian's location was a breeze to obtain.

The second part of the mission however... that was not such an easy task to perform...

When it came to killing Ian Roster, Leeza found herself battling with an unshakeable infatuation with her mark. She was not the only assassin out to get Ian, and once she had tracked him down... she witnessed him turn an entire six-man team of killers into a work of horrific art - spraying interior walls of a hotel corridor in buckets of claret and chunks of expertly carved human flesh.

The death squad were part of an elite government organisation, and despite having detailed files on their mark, they were clearly unprepared for the killing machine that was Ian Roster.

Leeza waited patiently in the shadows, preparing to make her move on her mark. She had spotted the six men in the lobby, recognising them as professionals immediately. With each member of the team branded with a rather unique tattoo on their necks, displaying allegiance to a guild of international assassins, she decided to take a back seat, stay hidden and observe, rather than interact and step into the firing line.

The eager, rather naïve group of assassins exited the elevator and charged towards Ian, wielding an assortment of blades and melee weapons. In a frantic yet skilful dance, Ian disarmed and dismembered each of the six men in a whirlwind of rapturous violence. The display of style and chaos struck a nerve inside Leeza and she immediately fell head-over-heels for the one-man creator of carnage and deliverer of death.

Two years later, their relationship thrived and the trails of mayhem the couple left in their wake were prolific... the talk of legends.

The fact that Ian had become infamous, kept him from being arrested. Criminal organisations saw him as an asset and were always willing to give him sanctuary when the heat was high. Ian's flair for carnage gave him the unique opportunity to be able to make a hit against an organisation one day, only to be hired by them the next - even when they were aware of his involvement.

In a city poisoned by greed and power, corrupted by violence and hate, feeding on the souls of the innocent, Ian Roster was an invaluable tool. For many he was the perfect weapon.

When Ian went to work, he was in his element, he was the perfect storm.

2

The darkest shadows of the night would normally prove haunting to a person... but not for Leeza.

For her the shadows were precious. They became her ally as she stealthily manoeuvred the streets, keeping herself mindful of the multiple security cameras which scattered the area. She found sanctuary in the shadows and was grateful of their presence. From the pools of darkness, cast down by the foreboding stature of the Deacon plastics building, she had time... time to breathe, to steady her excitement. Time to observe her lover as she waited to embark on their latest mayhem driven adventure.

The lobby's lights emphasised the outline of Ian's lanky, 6ft frame as he ascended the steps towards the large front doors. Constructed from armoured plexi-glass, the doors were designed to be near indestructible. Ian knew this... he also knew the framework bolstered around the doors was not up to the same perfectly engineered, impenetrable standard of the plexi-glass. He disabled the building's automated guardian systems as he approached the final step, a task easily achieved with a primitive remote device he had previously crafted at his kitchen table on a shoestring budget.

Ian plucked two small blue discs from his pocket, squeezing each one in turn until they gave out a faint activation beep. With an arm a professional sportsman would be proud of, he launched each disc at the building's entrance. The discs found their targets and attached themselves to the framework on either side of the large plexi-glass doors. They beeped again, this time the noise continued to sound for six seconds, and gradually increased in pitch.

Then they silenced. They changed from a solid blue to a pulsing green.

A maniacal smile surfaced underneath Ian's bright green beard as he ejected two custom made machine pistols from their holsters.

Ian also had his holsters made to his specifications, with

micro-hydraulic mechanisms which spat the pistols upwards from their casings and into his skilled and ready hands.

He aimed both pistols at the entrance and focused.

He twitched impatiently, watching the discs perform their display of illuminative signals. He focused on the colour changes, reading them like a familiar novel.

Ian nodded in synchronisation with the discs as they exploded simultaneously. A thundering crack echoed through the building as the blast sent the two doors spiralling across the Deacon Plastics welcome mat.

His smile widened. A surge of adrenaline flushed through his veins with torrential force.

The buildings' entrance had been transformed into an archway of raging fire. Thick black smoke elegantly cascaded into the lobby. A high-pitched ringing whistled through the air as ceiling tiles disintegrated and floated to the floor like delicate confetti caught in a soft whirlwind.

It was well publicised that Deacon Plastics had an unusually high security presence, so the pair were expecting some resistance - or as Ian preferred to call it: 'FUN!'

The lobby's security guard sat frozen behind his desk, crippled by fear. Blood had gathered inside his right ear - the tell-tale sign of a perforated ear drum, courtesy of Ian's explosive discs.

The stunned guard became transfixed by the smoke barrelling across the ceiling: dense, black clouds reminding him of a scene from an old action movie, the name of which had been erased from his bewildered memory.

Two hard thumps to the chest knocked him from his office chair, forcing his body to perform an awkward backwards somersault. The guards' head hammered against the tiled floor with an audible thud. His eyes rolled into the back of his skull like loose marbles in a tombola as he lost consciousness.

Reminiscent of a vengeful God storming through the gates of hell, Ian marched through the flames and smoke. His face was straight from the pages of a comic book, smiling like a maniac infected with a heavy dose of laughing serum. In steady anticipation, he kept his guns aimed towards the doors either side of the neutralised guard.

Ian had a rule: only shoot to kill when his own life was in danger. The guard had been caught unaware and Ian knew the two shots to his heavily armoured torso, plus the thunderous blow to the head, was enough to put him out of the game for a few minutes. If he were to rise again, Ian believed the guard would probably be questioning whether defending his employer's building for a pitiful wage... was worth chancing certain death?

In a world of madness, Ian felt that it was imperative to have rules to live by... but as an unarmed janitor ran into the lobby in blind panic, the spray of bullets from Ian's machine pistols showed that these rules were quite often broken, without any hesitation or moral dilemma.

A generous donation of the janitor's blood painted wild, arcing, splatter patterns over the mirrored walls.

Still clutching his mop, the elderly janitor flailed in the air as if his body had found a pocket of zero-gravity before finally falling to the ground like a rag doll.

A bucket of dirty water and used detergent rolled across the lobby floor towards Ian's feet. Without breaking stride, he rocketed the bucket into the mirrored wall with his right foot, showering the janitor in a brown, filthy slime.

'**Now, shall we go and burrrn this fucker to the ground, boy? You know you wanna, don't ya? Come on, boy, this is gonna be a hoot!**'

Ian rotated his head in an almost robotic motion. A small, purple, dragon-like demon floated over his left shoulder. The demon wore a blue denim waistcoat and a smile even wider and more maniacal than Ian's.

'You know I never fail you, man! I am going to enjoy this shit... just as much as you,' replied Ian, smiling at his purple friend, 'I live for this shit!'

Ian imagined many demons, they differed day to day, whether it be in colour, form or name, should they ever be granted with one - the only continuity in Ian's madness was that all the demons liked to cause havoc... just as much as he did.

'**LET'S SHOW THE BASTARDS HOW TO DIE!**' screamed

the frivolous demon as Ian began blasting his way into the next room - his volley of shots terminating two more confused armed guards as he entered.

The room was a showcase of products manufactured by Deacon Plastics, proudly positioned in large display cases that lined the perimeter of the room. Each display was beautifully illuminated with a warm, white light. Every product was accompanied by its own plaque, providing information detailing product specifications and purpose. A large u-shaped, blue sofa took position in the centre of the grand room, setting a partial perimeter around a colourless block of plastic that served as an ornamental table for scatterings of company brochures.

Ian continued his quest of carnage, utilising the large sofa as an improvised trampoline, propelling his body through the room. Effortlessly, he executed a stylish, acrobatic assault on four guards who had bumbled out of the elevator, each one too confused to ready their own firearms and return shots at their newly acquainted enemy.

Bouncing around like a jack-in-the-box made Ian less likely to catch a bullet himself, but the main purpose of his acrobatics was simply because he believed that he looked cool doing it… and to Leeza - he was 'the pinnacle of fucking-cool'.

She watched on, giggling in admiration and awe of his expertise.

Leeza followed Ian closely, holding her assault rifle tight to her right shoulder. Her head snapped to-and-fro methodically, leading the direction of her gun's barrel as she moved. She checked every corner, every doorway and every shadow, providing emergency backup for her man. Ian had taught her many combat skills and tactics to add to her already accomplished skillset. He taught her how to clear a building, how to move effectively and efficiently, how to react in close combat, but she rarely needed to utilise her training fully. She was always more of a spectator than an assistant, she knew Ian could deal with most scenarios instinctively… it was as if he had been born into this kind of work.

They were inseparable, spending almost every waking minute together. Next to one another, they looked like an odd couple, as if they had been incorrectly paired-up on a blind date. He had the face of an aging, crazed man - gaunt in shape and usually sporting a large gold-toothed smile. Although he was physically fit, he had the body of a man in desperate need of a meal. A shaved head and a long, braided beard which Ian often coloured with a plethora of dyes, complemented his funky image. He had a penchant for baggy jumpsuits in bold neon colours, along with heavy combat boots and black wrap-a-round sunglasses. His clothes, many sizes too big, hung loosely from his body. As he ran through the Deacon Plastics building, creating his unique whirlwind of raucous carnage, his baggy jumpsuit flailed behind him like a neon-green flag caught in a stormy gale.

Leeza was also lanky in frame but edged over her lover in height - standing at an impressive 6ft 4 and far too thin to be classified as slim. She had undergone many surgical procedures to lift and enlarge her breasts and buttocks. Additional money had also been frittered away on several operations of cosmetic facial reconstruction. Back in her escorting days, she always believed it was crucial to be as attractive as possible to potential clients and that was a tradition she never let go of. Leeza's surgical enhancements stood out a mile, even to the untrained eye: perfect hips, pouty lips and big silicone tits, Leeza had it all. Her love for figure-hugging cat suits had been something she had only discovered when she met Ian. She longed to look as cool as she believed Ian to be. She yearned to be his sidekick, his partner in crime, and she felt that her physical image needed to stand out just as much as Ian's.

He appreciated the admiration regularly transmitted by Leeza. Her sexual deviance pressed the buttons which violence and carnage could not reach, yet it never quenched his hunger for chaos. Ian's mind was plagued by demons and insanity, he was far too distracted to appreciate anything more than sex from his doting partner. He rarely acknowledged her presence, let alone returned any sort of admiration or affection, but Leeza did not care, she was happy to be his sexual slave and general lapdog. Her dwindling collective of acquaintances believed she now lived a shallow, worthless existence, one which was completely out of character for the once strong and independent woman. Despite their blunt, often vocal disapproval of her chosen partner, and the radical change in her personality, she found it impossible to wake from her trance - she was sucked in by Ian's presence.

All Leeza wanted was to come along for the ride and watch him work.

3

In a city poisoned by greed and power, corrupted by violence and hate, feeding on the souls of the innocent... Ian Roster was in his element, he was the perfect storm.

Ian continued to eradicate the numerous security staff scattered throughout the building's many floors, stacking up bodies with ease, making the art of war look like child's play. Anyone unfortunate enough to be left on the night shift, tending to their duties, soon met a bloody and violent end. To Ian, it no longer mattered if they were armed or not - if they were unlucky enough to be in his line of sight, they were a potential threat... and another lucrative mark to add to his unfathomable tally of kills. Ian's rule of 'only shoot to kill when his own life was in danger', had been completely ignored during his rampage... until he met a lighting repairman named 'Jeff'.

Ian encountered Jeff whilst clearing out the sixteenth floor. During a moment of rest, Ian and Leeza stumbled upon the repairman taking cover under a canteen table - he stood out like a lion in a library in the otherwise inorganic room. As the couple approached, the repairman crawled out from the table, held out his hand and announced himself. 'Hey there guys. I am Jeff... I... err... I maintain and I err... repair the lights!'

Amused by the repairman's pleasant and promiscuous greeting, Ian acknowledged the handshake and let Jeff be on his way unharmed. He reassured the repairman a guarantee of safety by means of a simple nod in admiration and a friendly pat on the back. For a fleeting moment, Ian had considered shooting Jeff in the ass as he walked away, just for his own comedic enjoyment, but he couldn't help but be charmed by the repairman.

A spectacular light show illuminated the labyrinth of corridors, stairwells and large rooms with strobing flashes of muzzle fire and a seemingly constant bombardment of explosions.

The purple demon loyally followed the couple on their journey, feeding on the death and destruction created by Ian and his deadly arsenal. A variety of munitions created a soundtrack of heavy thunder which accompanied the raucous laughter from Ian's small demon-friend. The demon's cackles spurred Ian on in his quest as he balled with laughter and screamed howls of crazed joy.

'C'mon Ian, kill 'em! Kill 'em all! You know you need this. You know I need this! They... they do not deserve to live, just look at how easy their pitiful lives come to an end. Their flesh tears so easily. Their heads roll, and their bodies drop to the floor without even putting up a fight... Their feeble life juices leave more of an impression upon this world than their lives ever have, haha-haaa!' The demon bounced upon Ian's shoulders, swapping from left to right and back again in a joyous, celebratory dance, his waistcoat flowing behind him in waves.

A plucky guard managed to dodge a hail of gunfire and charged towards Ian, wielding an empty shotgun like a club. The guard had carelessly spent the ammunition in his double-barrelled shotgun by plugging two large holes in the wall behind Ian's head. An outstretched left foot connected with the guards' nose, teaching him the error of his wasted rounds. Ian followed the kick by extracting a knife from his boot and plunging the blade through his opponent's throat.

The guard dropped to the floor as Ian holstered his guns before relieving his opponent of his shotgun and ammunition. He watched as the guard writhed around, retching and gargling on his own blood. He had attempted to clutch onto his shotgun, but his efforts were futile.

Ian shouldered a stolen bandolier, loaded the guard's shotgun and left the struggling man to bleed out - he felt no need to waste any shots on a man whose light was rapidly diminishing.

'Hey, what you waiting for? Finish that fucker off!' The demon bounced in front of Ian's face, whipping out an imaginary shotgun and firing two cartoon-like blasts into Ian's glazed eyes.

'He won't last much longer - he is no threat to me anymore!'

Ian raised his left hand and flicked the demon away from his path, ignoring the volley of cartoon shotgun blasts.

'Aww man, where is the fucking fun in that?' The demon's shotguns vanished, and a winged unicorn appeared between his legs. *'Oh well... ONWARD!'*

'Fun is my middle name. You won't ever be bored when I bring the pain!' Ian's reply was spat out with venom, his maniacal smile turned to a grimace. His psychotic, chaos loving personality was beginning to crack... and his little demon friend was nagging at his patience.

Leeza watched as Ian conversed in a one-way argument with himself, pausing for inaudible replies to his own words. She knew about the imaginary demons Ian carried around with him, she knew his sanity was questionable. On occasions she had tried to convince him the demons were simply a figment of his imagination, but her suggestions only agitated her lover. The last time she attempted to address his sanity, she found herself being strangled with a curtain tie. After escaping his rage, she thought it best to never mention it again.

It was always his derailed nature which reached inside of Leeza and sparked a hungry fire within... she adored him completely. Even though she was wary of his maniacal nature, she always found him to be charming... except of course if she were to mention the fictional creatures which he cosied up with.

Ian's demon cried out a belly laugh that echoed around the inner walls of Ian's skull. Ian too laughed hard and loud. The demon clapped his hands and vanished in a cloud of purple dust.

'Babe...' Leeza called out, 'the computer room is on your left!' She tossed over a hefty travel bag, crammed with explosive charges.

Ian scooped the bag out of the air and in one gliding, ballet dancer-like motion, delivered it through the glass doors of the computer room. He dropped the shotgun to the floor, before ejecting his pistols from their holsters once again. He turned and winked at Leeza, raising his arms, pointing the guns to the ceiling in anticipation.

Leeza read the signal and triggered the charges. The walls rumbled as a storm of reverberations rippled through them.

A shower of electrical sparks, flying shards of glass and slithers of airborne plastics glistened as they danced with red hot embers. The colourful choreography created a spectacular backdrop to Ian's jubilant pose.

Leeza watched on, frozen, stupefied in total admiration.

Ian's grimace fractured, his mouth broke into a smile so wide, it was clearly visible amongst the blackest shadows and strobes of blinding light. He revelled in the completion of his mission, he basked in the glory... shivered with excitement.

For Ian the mission was easy, creating chaos, havoc, and causing destruction was what he loved, it was what he was good at, it was what he believed he had been born to do.

Despite the adrenaline surging through his body and assaulting his senses, his brain still had time to question why there were so many guards on duty. Worry was not an emotion that plagued him, but he knew when something was clearly awry. A nagging thought that the whole mission could have been planned as a setup, certainly concerned him.

The purple demon reappeared on his masters' shoulder. **'What a fuckin' hoot, ay partner?'**

'What are you fucking wearing?' asked Ian, confused by the demon's sudden change of clothing - his denim jacket had vanished and this time he had chosen to cheer on his master's triumph dressed in an old military style jacket. 'You look weird, where did you get those threads?'

'Hey, I can wear whatever the fuck I want master...' The demon performed a pirouette on the business end of Ian's left-hand gun, then instantly traded his jacket for a long, flowing, white ballet dress. His head sprouted long, golden locks that curled as they fell almost weightlessly to the demon's waist. A large pair of naked breasts sprung from the demon's dress, bouncing in excitement. **'TADA! Whatcha think... fucker?'**

'This is messed up! This is fucking messed up, man! Am I going insane?' Ian shook his head in disbelief... beginning to question the level of stability inside his skull.

'Are you fucking serious?'

'IAN, C'MON! WE NEED TO LEAVE NOW, IT'S TIME TO GO!' Leeza signalled to her watch - time was running out.

The average response time for a police unit in the city was remarkably unpredictable. The slums were amok with criminals and there was barely any contrast in the 'business sector' either. The whole city was regularly flooded with alarm bells and gunfire, especially in the cover of darkness. However, a destructive assault the size of the one which Ian had just pulled off... that was sure to grab some attention.

Leeza had also begun to question the size of the security force employed by Deacon Plastics. She had expected a body count slightly higher than the usual standard, but not to the extent of the near a hundred corpses which Ian had created throughout the towering building.

Leeza's thoughts danced through possibilities, questioning what was so important inside the Deacon Plastics computer room. *What did a few hundred servers and hard drives of a plastics company contain that needed to be guarded by a small army of trained soldiers?*

She needed time to make sense of it, but with the wailing sounds of police sirens rapidly closing in on the building... time was clearly a luxury that had slipped from their grasp.

'I SAID, ARE YOU FUCKING SERIOUS, IAN?' The demon once again questioned his master, this time using an overtly aggressive tone, one he had never shown before.

'Hey, do you know who you are talking too?' Ian holstered one of his pistols and thrust his forefinger into the face of the angry demon.

'I don't think you realise who you're fucking talking too, man! You... you are fucking insane! You're nuts, crazy, cuckoo! You're talking to your-fucking-self, man!'

'What? What are you babbling on about? It is you who is nuts! Look at you in that ridiculous fucking dress!' Ian squeezed hard on the grip of his pistol, visibly trembling in anger. He shook his head frantically, then aimed into the face of the demon.

Leeza turned to see Ian's sanity unravelling like a ball of yarn tumbling down a stairwell.

A shiver rushed down her spine as she could see her lover crack, his eyes widening and his mouth brimming with frothing saliva. 'Ian, we don't have time for this. There is a chopper on the roof, we need to get on it and get the hell outta here!' Leeza frantically brushed a wave of sweat from her brow with the back of her wrist. 'IAN... STICK TO THE FUCKING PLAN!'

Ian flicked his head around in disbelief and glared at his partner. Never had she shown such blatant audacity towards him.

'IAN, COME ON, WE NEED TO...' Leeza's words were silenced in a volley of deadly gunfire, pounding through her skull. The once glamorous beauty became an eruption of bone and cartilage, swimming in a tsunami of blood and mucus. Leeza's body stood still and rigid as it parted ways with her fragmented head amidst a loud and obnoxious assault of high-velocity rounds.

Flashes of red and blue light began to flicker through the windows as the building became surrounded by a dozen police units. A burst of bright-white light blinded Ian as Leeza's body slumped to the floor in a bloody lifeless mess. The room came alive with huge beams from helicopter search lights.

'**IAN, WHAT HAVE YOU DONE? YOU'VE LOST IT NOW, MAN! YOU JUST KILLED THAT BITCH, AND NOW YOU ARE FUCKING SURROUNDED BY PIGS! LOOK, THEY HAVE A FUCKING CHOPPER! OOOOH, YOU... ARE...**' the demon waved his arms around in a frantic confusion, pointing in every direction in a random sequence. '**...GONNA... DIIIEEEE!**'

Ian turned his attention back to the demon, the barrel of his gun aimed back into his eyes. 'What did you mean when you said I am insane?' Ian's delicate grip on reality shattered, his face contorted through a range of bizarre animations and spasms. A fire raged in his eyes. He had no focus or even care of his impending doom: a heavily armed police team were storming Deacon Plastics and it would not be long before they reached his floor. The helicopter on the roof was his escape plan, but the route was almost certainly compromised and even if he could utilise his skills to battle his way through the waves of armed police... he had just executed his only pilot.

Ian froze… lost in a moment of panic. A single tear rolled down his right cheek as reality barrelled into him… yet something in his fractured mind still refused to acknowledge it.

'You're nuts Ian, totally fucking mental!' The demon jumped onto Ian's right shoulder and whispered into his ear. *'Didn't you know that, man? Did you not realise it? Don't you see, I am not real? I am in your head, man. I'm a figment of your fucked-up imagination, an extension of your own self. We all are… me an' the rest of my friends! You know it is true, people been tellin' ya for years now, man! You really think you can shoot me? HA! You have just killed Leeza! That woman loved you, and now she is fucking dead, just like you're about to be…* **unless we get the fuck out of here!'**

Ian watched the heavy rise and fall of his own chest for long, drawn out seconds.
He tried to calm himself… tried to refocus his mind.

'You're wrong, I'm not insane! Leeza is on the roof waiting. We're getting in the chopper, no problem. We're getting out of here, just like we always do!' Ian pressed the gun against the demon's left ear and laughed.
He thrust the weapon hard into the demon's face, sandwiching the little guy between the red-hot barrel and Ian's own head. 'You're wrong! I'm getting out of here... and yes... I am going to fucking shoot you!'
'NO, IAN! NO...' The demon's plea was silenced in a single

gunshot.

A splash of red filled the air.

Ian stumbled into the nearest wall and collapsed to the floor, his smoking gun landing beside him.

The argument had ended, and the demon had ceased to exist.

Every dog has its day.

Every storm finds its peace.

SECRETS OF SANITY
BY **CAROLINE WALLIS**

The Breaking Point of Successful Mortals

1

'The world is like an egg yolk, my friend!'

'Oh.... this is going to be good! How so? Really, please... please, would you be so gracious as to enlighten me with your latest misguided snippet of infinite wisdom?'

'Misguided? My dear friend, I speak quite simply the truth and how I see it. I cannot help that, at times, you fail to share my views of this world and the race which we call "humanity". We are not the great saviours of this world, as many would incorrectly believe us to be.'

'I am sorry, saviours? Just who believes that? Surely it is common knowledge we are the cancer of this planet... is it not?'

'There are many whom believe we are the supreme race, the most important things to grace this world. Some may not say it out loud, but they do believe it to be the truth... but it is not so. We... are like egg yolks!'

'Oh, come on! I am still waiting for your explanation of how we resemble a yellow sack of nutrients?' Rhys humoured Peter's ramblings - after working together for over a year, he knew it was the best approach. He could have attempted to shut down Peter's wild statement, but he knew it would have been futile, a waste of time and energy.

'Allow me to explain...'

'Here we go!' Rhys interrupted, as he stretched his well-rested limbs, let out a loud exaggerated yawn and adjusted his lips into an obvious wide and cheesy grin... all for the purpose of trying to get under the skin of his colleague.

'I am just going to ignore that childish display of ignorance, Rhys.' Peter kept his voice in his usual dull, flat tone, disguising any irritation caused by Rhys. 'So...' Peter paused as if for dramatic effect, '...as I was saying, my dear friend...' another pause, 'the world is like an egg yolk, and you are quite right that in saying "the world", I am predominantly talking about the huge collective of drones of none other than us... the human collective. We sit on a hot plate, cooking away, sizzling - ready to be consumed. If we sit upon the plate for just a little too long, over the harsh heat… we risk becoming tough and losing all our goodness and our flavour. If we are not given enough heat… enough time to cook.' a further dramatic pause attempting to encapsulate the attention of his disinterested colleague, '… we turn out all watery and weak, like a jelly. If we have too much pressure put on us, then we split, we burst… and all of what we are… just spills out and contaminates everything in our path.'

'Right… I kind of get what you are saying here, Peter.' Rhys rubbed a handkerchief across the back of his neck, soaking up a film of sweat which always seemed to be present. 'For once, it does kind of make some sense…'

'For once?' Peter was taken back by Rhys' comment, 'for once, my esteemed colleague?' Peter frowned as he tried to shrug off the deep cut of Rhys' remark.

'Yea, you do not always make strong arguments or analogies. Often you do not even come across as slightly coherent… but I do see where you are going here. That said, I don't quite see where today's strange analogy links in with Miss Ratcher in there?' Rhys nodded his head towards a zombified woman, shaking deliriously behind the two-way mirror.

'This would not be the first time my words have stretched your grey matter beyond the extent of its capabilities, you are easily perplexed, my dear friend!' Whenever Peter fired a derogatory comment or remark at Rhys, he would use the phrase – *my dear friend*. Rhys had noted the phrase would only ever be aimed towards him - he had never heard his colleague speak the words to others.

'Perplexed? Peter, your ramblings are not the great words of wisdom you perceive them to be. Any expressions of confusion or acts of perplexment, are nothing more than the understandable reactions to the gibberish and nonsense which spills from your lips on an all too frequent occurrence!' Rhys raised a gloating smile, pleased with his point scoring against his colleague.

'Enough of the chit-chat, Rhys…' barked Peter whilst glancing at his watch, 'time to see what this Miss Ratcher has to say for herself!'

Jessica Ratcher sat shackled to a table in the interrogation room, she was frightened, confused, a blubbering mess.

The forensics team had collected the necessary swabs, samples, and visible evidence from Jessica's body. They had allowed her a long shower before going into interrogation - but even after an uncomfortable, deep scrub, under the watchful eye of two stern female police officers, her skin still wore the stains of the man she was accused of brutally murdering.

No matter how hard she had scrubbed, no matter how much she lathered herself up in soap, no matter how high she turned up the heat and scalded her soft skin… the evidence of the slaughter remained, ingrained in her pores.

2

Time seemed to drag...

Seconds passed like minutes...

Minutes like hours…

The hands on the cheap wall clock seemed to be moving in reverse. It was no louder than the average mechanical timepiece, but its motions echoed around the eerily silent room. As the minute hand painfully inched its way around the clock's face, it could be heard like a deafening bell chime on the countdown to one's execution. The saying: 'so quiet, you could hear a pin drop' may be accurate, if it wasn't for the fact the floor was cushioned with deep, soft padding, and even a large concrete block dropping to the floor would be dampened to a tiny thud. The walls were also heavily cushioned, the table and chairs too… the room was quite literally a padded cell.

The soft interrogation rooms had not been designed for the purpose of protecting prisoners from hurting themselves - in fact, in the eyes of many officers they were more than welcome. Many police personnel believed if an aggravated prisoner were to take their own life during questioning, it would at least save on a truckload of paperwork. The sole purpose of the thick padding was to offer valuable protection to the interviewing officers – in case of any violent outbursts. The city's mayor claimed the criminal justice system could not afford to have officers failing to carry out their duties because of an injury, therefore each room had been transformed into bouncy, protective bubbles.

The decision making behind the padded interrogation rooms was another example of the times... in the eyes of law enforcement especially. Life had become all about statistics. Homicide statistics were particularly horrifying, the figures highlighting the alarming levels of crime thriving in a time of rapidly diminishing police numbers. A reported 81% of murders were left as unsolved cases. Conviction rates for the few solved cases averaged at 37%... the city was a cauldron of forgotten broth, left on the hotplate. The courts were next to powerless, and police had nowhere near enough manpower to bring peace and justice to the streets. Law enforcement had become the most dangerous way to make a living, and the government struggled to put enough people in uniform.

A dull reflection stretched the length of the smooth, gloss-white table, contorting the absent expression on Jessica's face like a novelty mirror placed in a fairground. Unlike the atmosphere at a fairground however, there was no light-hearted amusement inside the four walls of the interrogation room.

A gruelling hour had passed since Jessica had been brought into interrogation, dragged in like a limp doll by three heavily armoured police officers and then shackled to the padded table. The bracelets on her wrists were not tight enough to dig into her skin, but they were certainly restrictive, limiting many movements. A thick plasti-steel chain linked the two bracelets in harmony, keeping them fastened closely to the table. Jessica had been unaware of how frequently she would brush her side-parted, bleached blonde hair from her eyes... but with her new department issue jewellery hampering her arm travel, it had become obvious the movement was a more of a tic than an occasional habit.

Tears had streamed down her face for the first fifteen minutes. In the stale atmosphere of the pathetically air-conditioned room, the droplets soon dried to her cheeks, stiffening and solidifying against her soft skin. The familiar salty taste of her grief lingered on her quivering lips. A slew of emotions swamped her mind as the clock's noisy minute hand completed many full cycles. Her brain had gone into meltdown, reduced to a smouldering heap inside her skull. Her defences reacted. The grey matter repaired itself, bringing her back from the brink of despair... only for the whole process to repeat again and again... just for the pure sadistic joy. An undisclosed demon waited inside her head, messing with her nerves, plucking away at the increasingly frail strings of her sanity - or at least that was how she felt.

There was no way of Jessica knowing if anyone was approaching the interrogation room, no way of telling if someone was on the other side of the heavy, reinforced door… yet she just knew. A hunch perhaps? A strange sixth sense temporarily granted to her due to her heightened emotional state? Or perhaps, just a lucky guess?

She turned her attention to the electronically bolted door and waited for the audible signature of the locking mechanism. An almost tuneful sequence of melodic beeps sounded before the door slid open in a contrasting whisper. Two men entered the room, walking in single formation. Both stood tall, neatly dressed and slim in build. The pair also had faces which looked tired, strung out, in need of a good meal… and perhaps a heavy dose of caffeine to perk up their weary eyes.

'Miss Ratcher? I am Detective Peter Clay, this is my associate, Detective Rhys Black.' The first, slightly shorter one, wasted no time in introducing himself and his colleague, giving names and ranks before they had even neared the table. 'We are going to be asking you a series of questions' he continued. 'We will require your full cooperation, is that understood?'

Jessica nodded gently in response. She continued to tremble as the second detective sat down directly in front of her. He wore no emotions as he went through the necessary legal procedures and formalities. Jessica tried to take it all in, but even the hour-long wait had failed to calm her nerves. She was aware of the detective's words, she could hear his deeper than average voice droning in the back of her head, but she could not focus on it. Instead she became fixated with her metallic-blue nail polish which she had been subconsciously attacking whilst waiting in solitude. The metallic paint was a rather unique shade and very unusual in its composition: it had only ever been produced by one company. Government officials found it to contain traces of illegal squid inks, and subsequently its manufacture was criminalised forcing the producers out of business. Jessica had obtained a small stash of her favourite blue varnish and stored it in her office, but she knew the illegal nail paint was not the reason for her arrest. Her nails were not a concern for anyone in the interrogation room, other than herself… but it did make her curse her friend for buying it for her. The last thing she wanted was to have a charge of 'possession of contraband' added to her brand-new arrest sheet.

She considered blowing the miniscule flakes of nail polish from the table-top, but she was concerned that in doing so, it would only draw unnecessary attention to it, despite the very slim chances of either detective having any knowledge about the legality of the blue varnish. She tried to blank the thoughts and concentrate on the words of the detective, but it was not easy.

In her mind, the legal process seemed to drone far longer than the hour-plus wait she had endured before the detectives had entered. She had become aware of every passing second, even without focusing on the loud clock on the wall.

Once the legalities were finally out the way, an awkward silence fell on the room for three, long minutes. She knew the detectives delay in the questioning was merely a tactic to make her sweat and act out. They wanted to make her panic and hopefully spill some information they could use, obtain vital evidence with minimal effort.

Jessica may have been distraught, but she was not about to step into the firing line.

'I know what you're doing, you're trying to intimidate me… scare me!' Jessica pushed her head up high and proud, almost looking down her nose at them, attempting to mask any signs of being affected by the silence.

'Intimidation is not a word we like to throw around so liberally, Miss. We try our best to serve the public and bring the criminals in, to serve justice. Now, please allow me to first address that particularly touchy topic, before it becomes a pointless debate…' Peter coughed, clearing his throat, 'by acknowledging the high crime rates and the overwhelming pressure our criminal justice system faces. Therefore, I am sure you will be keen not to try our patience and drag this process out.' Peter's tone was calm yet direct, having faced off in many debates in the interrogation room, he wanted to quash any conversations about the city's strained police force before they began to concentrate on the delicate matter of questioning.

'Miss Ratcher, we really do have no need for this interview to cascade into the early hours of next week. The evidence against you is enough to bring you to justice… this is more of a formality. We are simply ticking boxes, crossing the 'T's' and dotting those 'I's' as it were. So, if you could just make it a lot less painful for yourself and tell us why you murdered Earl, my colleague and I can go home to our families, and you… you can get out of this room and settle down for the night. Quite frankly, you look in need of a good rest!' Detective Rhys Black had a cheerful tone to his voice, calming and friendly – he felt there was no need for aggressive questioning.

'I did not kill him! How... how could I possibly do that? I woke next to him and he was already fucking dead! His blood… his blood it was everywhere! Oh my… his blood!' Jessica scanned her blood-stained skin and fell to pieces all over again, the strength she had managed to muster crumbled in a fraction of the time it had taken to rebuild it.

'That is Earl's blood on your skin, Miss Ratcher! You do know who Earl is don't you? You do remember?' Detective Peter Clay pointed towards the stains on Jessica's arms, the tone in his voice less calming than his colleague's, but his manor was still soft and controlled.

'You know I remember who he is!' She lowered her head and questioned her tone, trying to be mindful of her emotional state. 'I just don't know what happened. I just know it wasn't me. I mean, it couldn't have been me, not in a million years... no way.'

'Your fingerprints were all over the body, all over the knife which had been thrust, again and again into his ribcage. He has been stabbed, not once but multiple times, puncturing his lungs… like a…' Rhys paused, looking at the ceiling, searching for words '…like a damn pin cushion! It's the same knife you used to slice his throat after the attack, finishing the job and ending his life. His blood… it still stains your skin, it's under your fingernails. Medics say the tests confirm it is indeed his blood. Were you to be found still holding the murder weapon, our officers would have shot you on sight… so please, I implore you... please think yourself lucky here.' Compassion poured out of Rhys as he tried to make eye contact with the increasingly distraught interviewee, he could tell she was not putting on an act, he could see her trembling in pure, agonising fear. It was clear she was at breaking point.

'Lucky? How am I lucky? To be sitting here? This was not me! I didn't do this... I... I couldn't! You must know... please, you must know... there is no way it was me. Please?' Jessica shook wildly, blubbering and snivelling as she pleaded with the detectives.

Suddenly, Jessica screamed out.

Her torso jolted forward violently.

She slammed her head hard into the padded table.

Her nerves shattered.

Her body began to convulse and spasm as if she had been possessed by something unholy.

The detectives jumped backwards from their seats and watched on in shock.

'FUCK! MEDIC... MEDIC!' Rhys screamed out to the room's array of microphones as he leaped forward to rush to Miss Ratcher's aide.

Peter grabbed Rhys by the arm and pulled him away from the table. 'Rhys, you know the rules, stand back! We are not to touch her. We cannot help her here. Come on, stand back!'

They watched on as Miss Ratcher's body wretched violently. Her arms jerked and tightened, contorting into almost inhuman angles under the restraints. Her shoulders twisted and rolled, thumping the edge of the table. Her legs kicked out and smashed the underside of the table. A mass of hair turned into a blur as her head slammed into the table again and again. Even with the soft padding blanketing the table in front of her, the multitude of blows to her skull was rapidly becoming a serious concern to her health.

The door opened, a four-man medical team rushed into the room and immediately removed the cuffs from Jessica's limbs. She continued to lash out wildly as they hoisted her from the seat and into an open space - limiting the chance of any further harm.

The two detectives hurried out of the interrogation room, leaving the medics to attend to their newly acquired patient.

'What was that? Some kind of... seizure? This is really going to make things awkward for us now!' Peter pulled two sticks of chewing gum from his shirt pocket and offered one to his colleague before taking the other for himself.

'You're all heart, Peter!' Rhys smacked his lips in disgust. 'Chew on them both… they might keep your mouth occupied for a minute or so!'

'Hey, that girl in there is a murderer! Our guys brought her in, they found her literally red handed. Why should I have heart? If she dies, it makes things a lot easier for us, you know this as well as I do!' Peter's cold remark was a hard pill to swallow, but a certain truth none the less.

If Jessica Ratcher were to die in the interrogation room, the case would be closed automatically, skipping the entire court process. The criminal justice system was overwhelmed, cuts had to be made wherever possible. The 'definitive investigations act' saw the number of homicide cases being closed had increased ten-fold in the five years since the law's approval by the courts. Any case where the accused was unable to stand trial - due to sudden death, would automatically be concluded and the case would therefore be closed. This also included any deaths caused by any actions from law enforcement officers during arrests, i.e. shot down during an arrest. Subsequently, the laws were seen by many as immoral, unfair, and wide open to corruption. A slew of incorrect results had been uncovered by campaigners, but the city's government felt it was a necessary step to help alleviate some of the pressures faced in a city at war with itself.

'Something is not right here, Peter, I can feel it. That girl in there… she is sweet and…'

'Woah, do you have the hots for that blood-soaked killer? My friend, the world is truly mad, but I had never realised you were going to be joining these delusional crazies! You have been under the heat too long, my friend. You truly are that egg yolk about to burst!'

'Enough with the egg yolk thing already!' Rhys scalded, 'something is not right here, Peter…' Rhys stared through the interrogation room window, observing the medical team at work. 'Something is just not right… I can feel it!'

Peter turned his back on his colleague and calmly made his way down the corridor, following the signs to the canteen.

'IT IS LUNCH TIME MY GOOD MAN. TIME TO GET SOME EGGS!' bellowed Peter, walking away from the drama of the interrogation room.

Rhys looked down at his feet. His boots were still sodden from standing out in the rain, waiting for his taxi before his unexpected, but not unusual, shift extension. He knew he was scheduled to work this day, but he was only down for fourteen hours... having lunch thirteen hours into the working day meant he could expect to be working through at least another three of flat-rate overtime... Rhys' day was only to get worse.

The detective raised his head and watched as Miss Ratcher's seizure continued.

'SOMETHING IS NOT RIGHT HERE, PETER!' Rhys called out to his colleague.

'IT NEVER IS, RHYS...

... It never is!'

3

The intensity of the ultra-bright lighting burned Jay's retinas - he always felt susceptible to any bright lights, but it was artificial lighting, like the ones lining the ceiling of the medical bay that really gave him the headaches. Every time he walked into the med-bay he could feel the pressure build up inside his skull. Each evening he would arrive home, shut himself in his study and sit in darkness. His wife would complain, saying he was imagining it - she blamed it on his late nights playing classic video games. She blamed it on too much television. She blamed it on masturbation. She even accused him of dreaming it up as an excuse to ignore her for an hour when he returned from work… that was partly true. Jay blamed it on the lights, he could feel their glare eating into his optical nerves.

His relationship with his wife was healthy and strong, he was often on the receiving end of her jokes, but he gave as good as he got. The couple's hectic work life meant very few hours of interacting with each other. The regularity of them passing in the wind was the hard reality of them both having high profile careers. Many marital discussions turned into petty, yet playful squabbles about how little their paths crossed, each one pinning the blame on the other.

Jay felt like he was married to his job most days, he had paid for a lengthy and costly legal battle to drop the title of 'Doctor' from his name to give him a bit of breathing space from his profession. The courts demanded he would need to change his whole career path to remove his title, meaning he would no longer be allowed to practice the profession he trained in… excelled in. Resilient, Jay poured vast amounts of money into solicitor's fees, stood his ground, and returned to being known as Mr. Jay R. Gest. Despite him dropping his title however, he still felt as though he was married to his job, and the long hours certainly contributed to his regular headaches.

'What's wrong, Jay? You suffering more headaches?'
'Yeah, more fucking headaches. I experience this immense, throbbing pain behind my eyes. It's stabbing into my brain…

like a pneumatic drill that has been switched to overdrive, controlled by a small child... completely incapable of harnessing its raw power.'

'So... you're saying it hurts, Sir?' Farah giggled at Jay's verbose analogy. The assistant loved to mock her superior, have a little bit of harmless banter with him - usually at his expense.

'Yeah, it is precisely what I am saying,' he massaged his temple, trying to ease the pain drilling through his skull. 'It's these fucking lights, they're the problem. I tell the wife... she doesn't believe me. I tell the maintenance team, they don't care. I tell the management... well, they're management, they never listen to me, I'm just a grunt!'

'You're not just a grunt, Doctor.' Farah gave him a playful wink, anticipating his reaction.

'Farah, please? Do not call me Doctor! Do you realise how hard I had to fight to rid myself of that restrictive title? I am a doctor by profession, but not by name. To you, myself, them... I am just a man doing my job. I do not wish to stand out. I do not wish to be treated differently. I am just like you!'

Jay spoke with passion - he truly believed his own words. He believed he acted like an average citizen, and he wished to be treated in the same respect as the next person. Whatever he told himself, whatever he believed - Jay carried himself with pride... he had a certain swagger, an air of confidence, a feel of importance. He was oblivious to it.

Ironically, by making a big deal of being known as 'Mr'... he inadvertently demanded and gained a new level of attention which did not exist when he carried the title of 'Dr'. Every time he met someone new, especially in the medical profession, there was a strong chance a conversation would ignite about his decision to no longer carry his rightfully earned title.

'Maybe you should change to tinted glasses, or even sunglasses?' she suggested, pointing at his spectacles protruding from his gown's pocket. 'The tint may help to diffuse the glare.'

'Tried that, Farah. Nothing works. It's these fucking lights!' Jay's pace through the medical department picked up a notch as his frustration grew. 'Farah...' he let out a heavy sigh of exhaustion '…tell me about this next patient, please?'

'In room 2011-B… we have a twenty-nine-year-old female by the name of Jessica Ratcher. The patient was arrested on suspicion of murder…'

'Suspicion?' Jay interrupted 'Is it likely…' he pondered his next words thoroughly for a few seconds, questioning the possibilities '…is it likely that she did it?'

'Obviously it is not my place to comment… but she was found lying next to the bloody corpse of a Mr Earl Beats. He had suffered multiple stab wounds to the chest and had his throat opened up by the same blade.'

'Wait, rewind… you mean this little thing? She is so delicate?'

'Yes, Jay… that delicate little thing in there!' she scoffed, slightly offended her superior would not entertain the notion of a seemingly weak female being capable of such a crime. 'Earl Beats is her lover as well as her partner in business. Miss Ratcher is a highly successful entrepreneur, and a rather wealthy one at that. She founded the Great Escape company, you know - the ones who offer trips to the man-made islands just off the coast. She also has her fingers in many other pies too… including some science labs, but I am not too familiar with the specifics on all of her ventures.'

'Oh yes, I have heard of Miss Ratcher! I'm not sure of her part in the project, but her science division claimed to have nailed human cloning a few years back. She was dragged through the courts and slammed by the press about the morality and potential dangers of cloning. She claimed the technology would only be used for medical purposes - transplants, and donors, bla bla bla... So, the authorities waded in and shut it down, fast. It was a prolific story. There were medical trials, and they proved to be… err… problematic - enhanced emotional reactions was one of the reported issues which plagued the clones, not always the nicest emotions either. I wouldn't agree she had nailed cloning.' Jay massaged his temple again, trying to soothe the pain. 'Human cloning… the devil's work if you ask me!' He stepped up to the inspection window and plucked the file detailing Miss Ratcher's medical condition from the hanger on the wall.

'What is her condition now?'

Jay handed the medical file to his colleague, allowing her to scan through the notes. 'I...err... forgot my glasses!' he smirked.

'That may be one of the causes of those headaches, Doctor!' she joked, pointing at the glasses protruding from his jacket pocket.

Jay ignored the remark and stepped in front of the inspection window.

'As you can see, Jay... she's in a coma...'

'Induced?'

'No, sir. She was in police interrogation and suffered a seizure. We are still trying to determine the cause... possibly severe stress. She slipped into the coma before the medics pulled her out of the room. Minor bruising around the arms, legs and minor brain trauma, not enough to account for her current condition.' Farah placed the file back in the holder on the wall and allowed a gentle sigh to escape from her lungs.

'You know what this means, don't you?' Jay pressed a small green button on the wall, inches from the viewing window. Room 2011-B flickered into light.

'Yeah, I do. It means if she does not wake up within ninety-six hours of her arrival, she will be declared non-responsive... announced deceased.' Farah wiped away the beginnings of tears from her eyes with her sleeve, she knew Jay would not approve of her empathy.

'Yes. There is more to it than that, however... once she has been declared deceased, the investigation into her lover's murder will be closed and her name will be tarnished forever, even if she is not guilty of the crime.'

'You really don't think that she is capable, do you? The evidence is pretty damning.... what makes you question it?'

'I don't question the case, the facts, or even the capability... I question the ridiculous laws used in times like this. How can one possibly close a case before the investigation is...?'

'Empathy, Jay? This is unlike you!' Farah interjected, surprised at her superior's reaction.

'I am not a robot! I just spend too many hours under these fucking lights, they affect me - makes me seem like I am cold.

107

I find myself infuriated by the outside world. I yearn to be at home, shut away from it all.'

Farah reached up to Jay's shoulder and rubbed his collar bone with a firm grip and noticeable amount of pressure. Her cheeky smile indicated that the gesture was intended as playful and affectionate.

'This is the way of the world we live in … often it just isn't fair.' Her cheeky smiled widened and was followed by a soft, delicate wink.

'It's the way of this city.' He turned out the lights in 2011-B and looked at his colleague, still sporting the grin on her face. The lights above Farah's head glared at him, stabbing at the back of his eyes. He massaged his head again, more vigorously than before, trying to shake the feeling off. 'Day after fucking day, this city just isn't fair!'

4

Success can be measured in many ways. It can be measured by your lifestyle. By the area you live in. The clothes you wear. The places you eat. The company you keep. The car you drive... even the size of your office.

Jessica Ratcher preferred to keep her success low-key, she was not one to show off. She felt she had no reason to rub her money or accomplishments into the faces of others... to her, showboating was distasteful - a disgusting human trait. The only problem was, almost everything Jessica touched turned to gold. She had been a money-making magnet. Even when she tried her hand at something and failed, she still managed to put her unique spin on things and create a profit - often by exerting even less effort than she had poured into the original idea.

Jessica's office was a showcase of her success - the only place where she would reflect on it all, where she felt no shame in feeling proud of everything she had accomplished. Certificates were framed and hung in pride of place. A plethora of a awards for a variety of achievements. Cuttings from articles displayed in carefully crafted mosaics lined a brightly lit alcove in the corner. Photographic memories of her meetings with rich and famous personalities. Her many stories of success and triumphs decorated the interior walls of her office, an unusual snapshot of her composed, almost invisible pride. The furnishings were elegant, yet grand. In the centre of the room stood an elongate, four-foot tall sculpture, positioned on a slowly rotating plinth. It glistened elegantly under five ceiling mounted lights which cycled through a spectrum of vibrant colours, illuminating the single word, carefully chiselled out of an exotic crystal. A single word: Ratcher.

To anyone who did not know her, the office could be a display of narcissism... however, everyone who did know her, knew that Jessica Ratcher was far removed from that assumption.

Ross' dirty blonde hair flopped in front of his eyes as he sat hunched over the desk. His thoughts lost for a few seconds in the patterns journeying along the length of the dark wood, a material which had become an exotic rarity in these times. Aside from the large sculpture, the office furnishings were of the usual modern standard, created from man-made materials. The long desk sitting at the back of the room was also different, it was intriguing to him. It once had life, once stood proud, strong... a living entity.

'I offer my sincere apologies, Ross. I know how much she means to you!'

'I appreciate your sentiment, Darrell.' Ross replied in a dull, insincere tone. His mind was distracted, his focus lay only on the woodgrain in the desk.

'I know this is a troubled time, but we need to think about the future of Miss Ratcher's empire and the Ratcher name.' Darrell signalled to the crystal sculpture in the centre of the room before placing a wad of paperwork on the desk. 'I have some forms here for you to peruse... and sign at your leisure...' Darrell danced his hand above the two small booklets, then immediately reflected on his inappropriate choice of words. 'Umm, sorry! Leisure isn't the correct word here... I'm truly sorry... it was careless of me to choose such thoughtless and hurtful words!'

'Please, save your grovelling, I know you meant no harm. I know what the papers are, and I will sign them in due course. Do not panic though...' Ross leaned forwards and tapped a poorly timed rhythm on the desk with his fingertips '...no need for hurrying. It's not as if she is ever going to be returning here, is it.' He scanned the papers - the two booklets were each separated by small bands across their centre. The first booklet was labelled: *Ratcher Inc. Power of attorney documentation.*

'Once signed, Ratcher Inc. will be in your hands, Ross... it is a big step...a sad step, but a necessary one, nonetheless!' Darrell exclaimed, with a tremble in his typically weak voice.

'You don't think I'm ready? I know exactly what this means. Once I have control, I will pull resources from all the pointless projects that Jessica saw fit to flitter the company's valuable assets on. I will push our efforts into the science divisions, gain the munitions contract from the government, and get the green light for our cloning program... we will prosper. We will grow... and we will thrive under my control... believe me!' Ross pulled a black fountain pen from the desk drawer and signed in the appropriate boxes on the last three pages of the first document.

'Are...are you not going to...' Darrell stuttered '... going to sign the second document, Ross?' the tremble in his voice became more audible as he pointed to the second book of paperwork. 'You said... umm... you said you would make me a partner. That is what you said. It is what you promised? I...I did everything you asked of me and will continue to do so, sir!"

'I said that, did I?' Ross clutched the booklet tight in his hands. The applied pressure in his fist saw his knuckles match the pale colour of the crisp white pages scrunching in his grasp. He pushed his feet against the floor and spun his chair round to face his associate.

Ross threw the booklet into Darrell's face, showering him in legal documents.

'Sir, what are you...?'

Darrell's question was silenced by a powerful strike to his throat. Ross had lunged forward and thrust the tip of his fountain pen deep into the larynx of his associate.

He frantically fingered his throat, trying to grab hold of the pen protruding from his neck. He spat out gelatinous orbs of phlegm and blood. Jets of rich claret spurted sporadically through his weak, scrabbling digits.

Ross tore the pen away from the punctured flesh, before thrusting it towards his victim once again - this time stabbing it into the black centre of Darrell's right eyeball.

The wounded assistant dropped to the floor in a gargling heap - thrashing out in an uncontrolled response to the attack.

After just a few seconds, his natural fight turned into involuntary convulsions and spasms. Froth bubbled from his quivering lips and spilled over his cheeks. Tortured screams forced their way out of his butchered throat.

Ross leapt from behind the desk, his eyes widened as his right boot slammed into Darrell's face. He burst into a frenzy, repeatedly stamping down with all his strength. The multiple blows silenced the screams and yelps of pain from the battered assistant. The fountain pen fired across the floor like a dart. The heavy boot of Ross' right foot continued to strike repeatedly - over thirty times, mashing bone and flesh into an unrecognisable, bloody pulp. The rage inside him did not calm until his energy was spent and exhaustion swamped his entire body.

Ross stumbled, drained from the brutality of his outburst. He hopped on his left foot for a second as he tried to shake off the numbness in his overworked right leg.

The office fell into an eerie quiet as Ross fought to slow his pounding heart. He observed the rapid convulsing of his chest. His lungs were working overtime, drawing in huge gulps of air and devouring all available oxygen.

He closed his eyes and tried to slow his burning respiratory systems.

'*I am Ross Ratcher! This company is rightfully mine…*' he whispered, leaning over the mass of red jelly on the office floor. 'This is my company now!' he spat, raising his voice aggressively. 'My sister would have let that fucking asshole, Earl Beats, continue to drag it along like a wounded dog... Not me! I will make it thrive… I will show the world who I am!' He continued, still fighting to calm his racing heart. 'I will build an army with the cloning technology my sister let slip from her grasp. I won't let the bastards stop me. They won't see it coming. I will rise… and I will conquer!'

A moment of calm washed over him as he leaned over the bloody mess on the floor, examining his grotesque creation, checking for signs of life.

There were none.

There was no need to examine the body to confirm his assistant's death, the possibility of surviving the onslaught would have been far beyond miraculous, but Ross found it relaxed him.

As his heartbeat calmed, he paced slowly, studying the office. He found himself displeased by the décor of the room, especially the large crystal sculpture in the middle of the room, He stared at the rotating piece and questioned its place in his newly acquired lair.

He returned to the bloodied monstrosity once again, leaning in even closer to it, checking again for signs of life. Still, there were none. He yanked at Darrell's left foot and dragged the lifeless body through the office, smearing blood and brains across the floor. He struggled with the dead weight as it seemed to turn into lead and anchor itself to the smooth tiles.

Ross persevered - heaving the body fifteen feet to the bathroom door.

The door opened automatically on his approach.

A stench of dead flesh and bodily wastes hit him like a hammer to the face.

'Aww, fuck!' He muttered, peering into the room and studying the ageing corpse left mutilated on the bathroom floor. 'Shit, Ross... I am definitely an improvement on you! You have seen better days, my brother!' He chuckled, talking to the decaying, bloated hulk sprawled on the bathroom tiles.

He squirmed and moaned as he slumped Darrell's lifeless body on top of the rotting corpse - a man who was identical to himself in almost every detail... Ross Ratcher.

He found himself transfixed by his blood-covered hands. Beneath the wet blood of his associate, dull red stains were ingrained into his skin.... stains from the claret which had been extruded from his first victim, just a few days before.

Ross stepped back into the office. The bathroom door closed behind him and he caught a reflection of himself in the window. The reflection was the perfect copy of Ross Ratcher, older brother of Jessica Ratcher.

Every feature identical.
Every freckle a carbon copy.
Every wrinkle perfectly in place.
Every strand of hair unmistakably dirty blonde.
Every familiar cloud of green...
...sparkled softly in his impeccable eyes.

Everything was exactly how it should be...
...minus all signs of emotion.

113

Ross returned to his desk and found a blood-free section of skin on the back of his wrist to wipe away the beads of sweat from his glacial face. He rubbed his fingertips together slowly, examining the texture of the blood which had gushed from Darrell's wounds. He brought his hand up to his mouth and tasted the blood... the fluid was almost cold on his tongue and seemed completely absent of any taste.

Ross pondered for a few seconds when the last time any flavour had passed his lips... he could not remember, but his brain nagged at him like he should.

He dismissed the confusing thoughts quickly, not wanting to be carried off into a pointless dream... it was time to focus.

He reached out to the intercom button on the edge of his desk, tapping the large white button with his bloody forefinger, and calmly requested two cleaning droids to attend to a spill in his office.

A gentle female voice eagerly acknowledged the request, then asked if he required any other services... Ross did not reply, he just sat calmly and let the intercom crackle fade to silence.

Ross leaned back in his chair, his arms hanging free, dripping with blood, forming small puddles of vibrant red claret on the office floor. He turned his head to the side, facing the closed bathroom door. Vivid pictures of the two dead bodies, lying together in a heap stood out in his mind - he smirked... but his smile appeared as if it had been painted on.

He stood and walked over to the large windows of the office, creating small trails of blood splatter as his hands continued to drip dry.

The view was spectacular, a maze of lights glowed in the city night.

He rocked back and forth on the balls of his feet. The vast skyline transformed into a reflection of his own face - it showed no signs of regret, no signs of guilt, no signs of emotion... his expression as cold as ice. His face was frozen, and his eyes were as cold and empty as his soul.

He was void of all emotion.

He stopped himself from rocking and stood motionless,

positioning himself in the best light so he could examine the perfection of the man in the reflection.

'I AM... THE NEW... ROSS RATCHER! THIS COMPANY IS MINE!' His voice echoed in the dead silence of Jessica's old office.

He continued to explore the reflection carefully, noting all the visible imperfections inherited from his donor as the echoing voice clung to the air.

He waited for silence to once again consume the office, time passed slowly, yet his mind raced.

'I will build a clone army, and I will conquer.'

He wiped his hands repeatedly down the front of his jacket, smearing the fabric in the blood of his latest victim.

Ross turned slowly, facing the rotating crystal statue in the centre of the room...

He froze, watching its rotation under the cycling colours from the lighting above.

'My name is Ross Ratcher... and I am in control!'

THE BREAKING POINT OF SUCCESSFUL MORTALS
BY **ANDREINA DIAZ**

The Journey of a Methodical Combatant

1

'Hyper-sensitivity'... that is what the doctors call it. That is what the specialists, the medics, the experts, the professionals, the quacks, call it. Waz called it... 'a fucking curse'. The ability to decipher, to analyse, to pick apart his surroundings in unfathomable detail. To examine the situation and a vast number of possible outcomes like a mathematical equation was a cause of constant stress and headaches. A network of nerves communicating in perfect synchronicity, triggering coded signals which would usually go unnoticed in the standard human brain... but Waz's nerves were alive with highly charged, furious electrical impulses. The rush of signals bouncing around the inside of his skull like a high-velocity ball-bearing, ricocheting off the bumpers of a pinball machine: a constant test to the walls of his sanity. He was not insane, far from it... he was a rational, logical, methodical thinker... and at times he hated it. If he could take a drill to his head and silence the chaos, calm the storm, he probably would... but the blood splatter on his clothes would seriously fuck up his day.

The heat in the dressing room was tedious... it nagged at Waz Older's focus, begging him to crack, to buckle, to break... but he was not going to allow it to happen - he could not afford for it to happen.

He could feel the sweat seeping from the pores on his freshly shaved head, but with his strong will, the perspiration became as easy to ignore as the noise outside the dressing room.

The wraps hugging his hands and wrists began to feel like part of his skin - the familiar tension from the layered fabric was comforting, he knew the importance of protecting his joints. He would always ask for his wraps to be done in the same way each time. If he was not entirely pleased with the wrap, he would tell his trainer to start again, and he was never too shy to mention it. On this occasion, his trainer had been instructed to repeat the procedure four times before it finally felt perfect for the fight. As frustrating as it was, his trainer never questioned the fighter, he just quietly removed the entire length of layered fabric and replaced it with a clean, fresh wrap each time. The movement in the fighter's wrists was crucial to his grappling, he loathed to feel constricted, seven rotations of his clenched fists would tell him whether he was going to struggle or not.

The routine was like many other tasks in Waz's life - a ritual which he had to follow. His highly active brain required him to place a tick in each box before he could comfortably move onto the next task. Once each box had been marked… he was ready to take on anyone.

Waz Older was at the top of his game: an undefeated, mixed martial arts world champion - gearing up to defend his world title for the fourth time. Under the 'wildcard rules', once a belt holder successfully defends the title in three consecutive fights, a name would be drawn at random from the Amateur Leagues. The random selection would be given the opportunity to challenge the defending champion for the title. The rule was passed following the rapid decline in popularity of male fronted competitive sports. The move was a big gamble, one which resulted in many amateur fighters having their careers cut short due to lacking the experience to take the punishment from an opponent at the very top of the rankings. However, the rule also threw a few shocks into the world of professional fighting, with a handful of plucky amateurs walking away with titles and huge purses from their shock victories, but that event was a rarity.

Waz won his belt the hard way, battling through the amateur rankings, rising to professional level. A fast and impressive climb to claim the title of World Champion followed as his skills and endurance improved and he became a modern legend. He had never lost a fight, never even suffered a draw… but that didn't make his journey an easy one. He took his fair share of beatings whilst claiming his victories and he was yet to find an opponent capable of bettering him.

In the ring, against a hungry amateur, anything could happen and he knew it. The chance of a shock defeat did not faze him, his focus was on par with his refined skillset. He knew every fight was a new lesson, there is always something to be gained from an opponent, even an amateur. He knew exactly how he would have felt had he been given the wildcard opportunity as he fought his way up the ladder. Such opportunity would have fed his hunger, fuelled his ambitions. He would be brimming with energy and enthusiasm. The adrenaline rush would gift him a boost of power that he never knew possible. He knew he could not let his guard down and knew he had to prove he was still the best in the world.

If Waz won the wildcard match, he would go on to fight the National second seed. If the challenger triumphed, the amateur would then go on to face the World Number Two... an international previously defeated by Waz six months prior. If the champion fell, his decline would be rapid as the rules stated *'no rematch for two years'*, in the world of a fighter, that was a career death sentence.

Waz Older knew the risks of a wildcard match, but it did not faze him. He sat on the bench in the dressing room, ignoring the heat, staring at his wraps, his mind completely focused and calm.

'Hey boss... it's time!' announced the trainer as he handed the fighter his signature green gloves.

2

A subdued crowd was not unusual for a men's bout, the seats in the stadium were packed, but the majority were waiting to see the headlining fight: Samantha Cantenbury versus Aries Di-Rosi. The Sigari Sports Arena was a premier venue which had almost completely stopped hosting male-combat events. The Cantenbury/Di-Rossi fight was a hot ticket and one which had occurred with little notice, making the Older/Miller fight the only match of calibre available to tack on to the billing. The arena had sold out, thirty-four-year old Waz had never stood before such numbers but it didn't shake his nerves, he was a solid pillar of focus.

The large audience had become a concern for his opponent: Simon Miller, a six-foot hulk of a man. His shaved head and an ample collection of tattoos sprawled over his torso, along with his impressive frame - to some, he carried the appearance of a brutish animal, but the image was an inaccurate scar on his personality. Simon was in fact a quiet and timid family man. The biggest audience Simon Miller had ever seen during his seven-fight career was a mere thirty-seven, and most of them showed up to cheer on the opponent. His matchup with the mighty Waz Older told a very similar tale – the small pocket of fight fans in attendance to watch the men's bout was marginal. Those who had shown an interest in Simon's fight were largely there to support the champ... most had never even heard of Simon Miller before he was drawn as a wildcard.

The champion knew his opponent, he had studied tapes of the last three Miller fights, he would have preferred to have seen more, but the last three were the only ones recorded. Miller was a competent wrestler, but an excellent brawler - his upper body strength was clearly superior to Older's, but his groundwork was his big weakness. Stamina could also be an issue as Miller had never fought beyond the second round, racking up three superb knockout wins, one win by submission after flooring an unguarded opponent and managing a sufficient arm-lock... and three first-round losses, each by submission. Wrestling was certainly the way to play it against the hulking opponent. Waz figured going toe-to-toe was a bad idea, he felt confident he could block, deflect, and counter many of the brawler's strikes... he certainly wanted to avoid taking any blows on the chin.

The array of speakers in the arena snapped into action...

"GOOD EVENING FIGHT FANS! ARE YOU READY FOR A SPECTACULAR TITLE BOUT, HERE IN THE WORLD FAMOUS SIGARI SPORTS AREEEEENAAA?" The announcer's jubilant introduction echoed around the room but failed to make a large impact amongst the crowd.

The announcer continued, defiant of the disinterest in the crowd, welcoming the panel of judges, the ring-girls and finally, the two mixed-martial artists as they entered the arena to their chosen music. A small scattering amongst the crowd erupted, and the buzzer sounded for the fighters to take their places in the centre of the ring.

Waz Older stood in white trunks wearing green-gloves.

Simon Miller wore black trunks, and red gloves.

The referee firmly talked the men through the rules before they touched gloves. He thanked the fighters for their obedience towards the sporting traditions and gave the signal for the title fight to begin.

Miller waded in like a wild bull. His nerves showed with his sloppy and clumsy footwork, making it easy for Older to dodge each eagerly thrown heavy strike.

Miller carried the stance of a boxer and looked like he would be more at home wearing a pair of heavy gloves, duking it out in a traditional boxing ring.

The two fighters danced around the ring for the whole duration of the first round. Miller failed to connect any strikes and Older only threw two punches, both heavy left-uppercuts connecting with Miller's unguarded ribs. The second punch should have been a game changer, the blow connected perfectly. Waz felt bones buckle and break as he connected, but that was with a minute to go in the first. The well thrown strike only seemed to enrage the eager challenger, as he came back at the champion with a flurry of heavy straights that certainly pressed Waz's perfect guard... but failed to be anything more than a test of the champion's ability.

Miller's inexperience was obvious.

Waz moved around the ring with ease. He watched his opponent's muscles tense and his limbs contort as he performed each failing strike. The champion could read the face of the challenger like a paint-by-numbers book.

The first round may have predominantly been a boxing match, but Miller had come out kicking in the second, despite possible broken ribs. He showed his hunger with a barrage of high kicks aimed at the taller champ's head. Each kick failed to connect, leaving the challenger open to two textbook leg sweeps that left him floored and stunned.

The second bell sounded, and the fighters returned to their corners. Waz could see the exhaustion in Miller: it was clear the challenger was unprepared to pace himself.

Every punch thrown at Waz was bomb, ready to take his head off. Every kick powered towards him with the speed to break bones. Every grapple was a wrestle for life, clutching and grabbing with very muscle. Simon Miller had executed every move with maximum effort, he wanted the win badly... he was desperate, too desperate.

The second round went by in a flash. Waz's trainer congratulated him on another round of avoiding the offensive fighter. He too could see the champ was wearing the over-eager opponent down, and the inexperience was easy to predict and counter.

Waz spat the accumulation of excess phlegm into the corner bucket before guzzling ice-cold water from his flask. He stretched his limbs and rolled his shoulders forward, his joints cracking under tension.

He gazed across the ring and made eye contact with his opponent.

Miller was slumped in his corner, the look on his face said it all... he was already beginning to give up. There was no belief he could beat the reigning champion... in his own mind he was already defeated.

Waz had seen the look many times before, but this time

something was different.

The challenger looked tortured with disappointment. It was obvious Simon was about to break, and for some reason Waz could feel his pain... but unlike many fights before, the opponent's pain did not trigger the usual 'now let's finish this' hunger inside... instead, Waz experienced an emotion he had never known his methodical brain was capable of...

...he did not know it, but the emotion was pure empathy.

Waz blinked slowly, blocking out the bright lights of the arena. When his eyes reopened, his confused brain had pressed down on a pause button. He could still move, still function, but everyone, everything else had been frozen in a moment in time.

He scanned the arena, picking out only a handful of interested faces amongst the huge crowd. He read the dull expressions of the majority and thought to himself... *'These guys are fight fans? They have come to see a fight, not the humiliating defeat of an unknown'.*

The disinterest in the arena was alarming... thousands of faces stuck in mid-conversation, playing with their communicators, reading the event programmes, waiting in line at the busy bars scattered around the arena, *picking their fucking noses...* anything other than watching the men's title fight before them.

The lights scattered around the arena performed a ballet of colour, creating an atmosphere hoping to encapsulate the audience - lighting which should have instead lit up the action from the two combatants slogging it out in the ring.

The judges sat at their ring-side table seemed more interested in the two ring girls parading their heavily modified assets, than the action they were being paid to analyse. Instead of judging the two fighter's conditions, their eyes collectively fixated on the scantily-clad, young bodies climbing through the ropes to introduce the third round. The ring girls themselves were hard to read, they wore well practiced, fake smiles that were carbon copies of any previous appearances, they were true professionals.

In the stands, even the hot-dog sellers showed no signs of

interest in the fight, not that they had any investment in the outcome, but it was the bored expressions on their faces which summed up the mood perfectly.

Sat across from Waz, a man covered in sweat. A man pumped full of soaring adrenaline raping every drop of available energy. A man exhausted, drained, dehydrated. A man given an opportunity, given a chance to change his life, to become something. A man with a chance to prove his worth to not only his friends and family, but to himself... a chance which he may never have again.

Simon, the once hopeful amateur, now a tired, fading wreck... after only two rounds in the ring.

The buzzer sounded for the third round to begin and Waz awoke from his daze. He walked to the centre of the ring and touched gloves with his opponent.

Once again, the referee signalled for the fight to commence. This time Waz went straight on the offense, hammering Simon with powerful kicks to the right thigh. Simon managed to swerve the fifth consecutive kick and counter with a surprising left hook to the jaw, rocking the champ for the first time of the fight.

Waz staggered backwards, away from the challenger. He could feel the swelling on his cheek instantly. He shook his head and stared into the eyes of the challenger, he could see a slight glimmer of hope, but Miller's excitement was shortly followed by a realisation he had failed to follow-up on the successful strike - giving the experienced World Champion a chance to gather himself.

Waz drove forward into his opponent's torso and lifted Simon from his feet, powering his shoulder into broken ribs before slamming him to the mat.

The challenger landed with a heavy thud, a combination of momentum and his own weight had punched the wind from his chest, and before he knew it, the champion had hooked him in an impenetrable leg lock.

Waz watched as Simon Miller struggled to break free from the lock, but the champ knew it was a hopeless fight. Waz Older's leg-lock was his signature move, he had mastered it and used it to take out numerous amateur and professional fighters.

Simon Miller began to go limp...
He began to accept defeat.

Waz could feel the fight in his opponent's body fade. He could see the defeat in his face come flooding back. He could see tears form in his eyes.

Waz pulled out of the lock and manoeuvred himself on top of the challenger, pinning him between his legs.
He raised his arms, preparing to reign down a series of left-handed hammer fists...
...but then...
...he paused...
...he hesitated...
...he saw a glimmer of hope return in Simon's eyes...
...and he gently nodded to the challenger in admiration.

Simon delivered a right hook to Waz's chin. The force of the blow shook the champ and he tumbled from the amateur's body, opening the doors for a comeback.
Waz staggered to his feet, almost falling as he shook the strike from his head.
He watched as his opponent leapt to his feet. The fire in Simon Miller's eyes reignited with a vengeance.
Waz threw a series of uncharacteristically weak right hooks, which the challenger easily slipped.
Simon returned with a powerful straight-right, which seemed to come at Waz in super slow-motion.

The champ's brain once again froze time.
His eyes studied the arena - the interest in the fight had spiked.
People were focusing on the ring.
Judges were out of their seats.
The ring girls held each other in a clinch of anticipation.
The large room was excited by the possibility of a fallen

champion… even the spotlights were now focused on the hopeful amateur.

The fire in Miller's eyes was now raging, burning with scorching reds and ambers. A smile was beginning to appear in the creases of his grimace.

Waz's brain computed the situation, moving through multiple equations at its usual speed of light.
He could see the challenger had over-reached and his muscles were stretched to their full extent.
He could see the energy shift from Simon's feet, throwing himself off balance.
The challenger had committed himself completely to the powerful strike.
Waz had an opening.
All he needed to do was raise his right arm, parry the straight, and step to the left. The manoeuvre would throw the challenger's balance completely and leave a wide opening for a career ending left-hook.

Waz admired the hopeful in freeze-frame, stuck in a potentially life changing moment.

The champ smiled and closed his eyes. He dipped his right shoulder and bit down on his mouth guard.
The straight connected and sent Waz airborne across the ring. He landed flat on his back, sprawled across the canvas.

Waz's vision blurred, he could only just make out the outline of the referee rushing to his side and begin the countdown.
He rolled his head on the canvas and another blurred outline came into view. He concentrated on the hulking opponent standing behind the referee, he could not make out his face… he did not need to. Waz could sense the expression appearing on the amateur.
He closed his eyes and listened... as the count reached ten.
The image of his opponent standing, watching, waiting, floated through his skull as his brain lost all communication

with his body.

Despite the enclosing darkness in the champ's mind...the expression on Simon's face was clear...

...The unmistakable thrill of the win.

3

Following the match Waz Older attended the customary post fight press conference. A small gathering of spiritless journalists had been pulled together to quiz the two fighters about the action in the ring.

An uncomfortable pause at the start of the conference filled the room as neither the journalists nor the two fighters had anything to say about the evening's *shock defeat.*

Waz sat calmly in his chair examining the dormant media representatives as they blankly stared back at the two battered fighters. He looked over at his opponent, witnessing the bewildered look on his face as he struggled to gather himself following the triumph.

Finally, a young journalist showed willing and began the questions, asking the former champ, 'Waz Older, did you feel that you were unprepared for the brute strength of the challenger?'

Waz gazed into the eyes of each journalist in turn, assessing their attention levels. He counted twenty-two sleepy eyes, all lost in their own worlds, rather than showing interest in the thoughts of the two fighters. Waz had been to many press conferences before, he knew that for everyone concerned it was simply a routine… everyone except Simon Miller that is. For Simon, this was his moment of glory, his time in the spotlight… no matter how dimly lit it proved to be.

Waz stood from his chair and immediately announced his retirement. He turned and faced the new champion and shook his hand firmly before informing the press that he felt he was no longer at the top of his game. He told them a new, more worthy champion had risen from obscurity. He said Simon was ready to hold his own against any challengers, and he was sure the new champion was capable of greatness.

Waz turned his back on the journalists and left the room to a small eruption of excitement, begging the former champ to explain his actions.

Simon Miller was a promising fighter, Waz would be the first to admit it. Now he had claimed the title, he would benefit greatly from experienced trainers who would be anxious to work with and fine tune the new Mixed Martial Arts World Champion.

Waz had experienced his moment in the spotlight, he had been the undisputed, undefeated champion of the world. He had achieved everything he had committed himself to, but now was the time for a new champion… now was the time for Waz to be the family man his wife had begged him to be.

He knew Simon Miller had never been a lucky fighter, and his past was littered with injuries and missed opportunities, but now was his chance to shine.

4

The carpark was cold and silent, but a raging thunderstorm continued to clap violently inside his head.

Highlights of the fight played through Waz's head at a thousand frames per second. The image of Simon Miller's gloved fist, powering towards his eyes left a vivid concept imprinted on his imagination.

Waz loved to paint, it helped him unwind, it helped him relax, but most of all, it helped him regurgitate the chaos inside his skull - left there as a by-product of his hyper-sensitivity. His paintings were photo-realistic, the attention to detail was precise, down to each individual hair follicle. He mastered reflections, refractions of light, recreating colours to the exact hue, replicating the exact spectrum in the original image.

He loved to paint, but if his work did not turn out to be exactly how he wanted, the piece would never see the light of day. He would never show anyone his work until he was completely satisfied... and when you are a hyper-sensitive painter, a large amount of your work ended up heading straight for the fire.

A clear picture stapled itself to the front of Waz's mind: A man throwing a green gloved fist, complete with intricate creases in the fabric, signs of wear from the fight, showered in beads of sweat and snot, smothered with grease. The man stands alone in the ring, strong and proud. In the background: glaring spotlights, camera flashes, judges on their feet, a plethora of cheering and applauding audience members surround the ring... all shocked by the outcome of the evening's events.

The image is precise in every minute detail... but then it fades... it transforms.

It morphs into a more relaxed style of painting. The man with the glove, the fighter, is a shorter, yet larger man than before. He stands looking at his glove with a steady focus. The glove is red in colour. The hand is relaxed, unclenched, open. His back is turned. His expression is hidden from sight.

The ring resembles a boxing ring. The canvas blurs into a beautiful blue abstract image of the city. The table of judges and the huge crowd seem to fade further into the distance, becoming a sea of unrecognisable faces. The arena mutates from the huge spectacle of the Sigari Sports Arena, into a smaller single storey arena, more of a warehouse than a multi-billion credit complex - an arena that every fighter recognises as the beginning of the road.

A loud bang echoed through the carpark, resonating through the concrete and steel.

'What the fuck was that?' questioned Waz as he was woken from his dream.

A second loud bang followed... and then nothing... just silence.

Instinctively he clenched his fists and listened out for sounds of commotion to accompany the two startling sounds. The sounds were all too familiar when you live in the city.

'Was that... gunfire? What the fuck?' Waz spoke out loud to himself. He caught his reflection in the car window. 'You're imagining it, Waz. It's just a car door or something... and now you're talking to your own fucking reflection!'

Waz chuckled to himself, the Cantenbury/Di-Rossi fight was over, it too had ended in the shock defeat of the more acclaimed fighter. He figured the noises may have been someone blowing off steam after the shock of the big fight.

Waz had been in the dressing room during the women's fight, he was recovering from the heavy knockout blow delivered by Simon Miller. He had little interest in the Cantenbury/Di-Rossi brawl - he felt it was a manufactured bout, put together by greedy agents after a petty argument, but he had to remind himself that his fight was also one constructed from a business decision, rather than a ranked match.

The remote to Waz's car was temperamental, it was the one thing which really ground his gears, day in, day out. Every time he pressed the button, he prayed it would respond... but nine times out of ten, it would play dead.

'Fucking thing!' he muttered to himself.

'Excuse me, Mr Older? May I have your autograph?' requested an unfamiliar voice from behind.

'Sure thing!' Waz sighed. He reluctantly forced a smile and turned to face the voice… he hated giving autographs.

A sharp, powerful blow met with Waz's throat, crushing his larynx. He immediately fell backwards against the car and slid down the bodywork to his knees.

A shorter, long-haired, bearded man stood before him, his body shaking fiercely in anger. His eyes covered by wrap-around sunglasses, his mouth foaming with venom.

'YOU' the attacker called out. 'You ruined me, Older… I was gonna fight YOU! I was meant to have my shot at the title. I have trained relentlessly… I was going to win!' The man paced back and forth.

Waz felt his airwaves close and his brain beg for oxygen.

'Me, Rick Finley! The National Second Seed. I fought hard to get where I am… I am your next opponent, but you took that from me! Now I have taken your life from you. That fucking nobody up there, you let him win. He will go on to fight that foreigner, but it should have been me fighting next… ME AND FUCKING YOU!'

Rick Finley's rant failed to sink into the former champ.

Waz was in panic, realising the severity of the attack. As a fighter he knew where to strike to kill, every fighter does.

He desperately clambered around on the concrete as he felt his brain shutting down…

He closed his eyes… and tried to fight the walls closing in on him, but the darkness was approaching once again, only this time there was no referee counting him out.

An image stayed with him to the very end…

… it was vivid and real, down to the finest detail:

A man throwing a green gloved fist, complete with intricate creases in the fabric, signs of wear from the fight, showered in beads of sweat and snot, smothered with grease. The man stands alone in the ring, strong and proud. In the background: glaring spotlights, camera flashes, judges on their feet, a plethora of cheering and applauding audience members surround the ring... all shocked by the outcome of the evening's events.

The image is precise in every minute detail...

...but then...

... it fades...

THE JOURNEY OF A METHODICAL COMBATANT
BY **TANIA TAYLOR**

Judgement of the Faceless

Part One

We join our gallant heroes as they blaze across a section of the city's monstrous overpass. In their wake they leave shreds of smouldering tyre rubber, clouds of dust and plumes of blue smoke. Their frenzied motorbikes thunder and roar along the sluggishly lit roads. High-revving soundtracks scream from their tortured engines. Neon light trails scorch the atmosphere like a high-octane disco fed on amphetamines.

Two strangers, cloaked in black motorcycle suits, hidden beneath the oil-coloured visors of their helmets.

To one another they are partners, yet they never meet. Each have never faced their associate, not outside their missions of the night. They know nothing of one another's life out-of-hours, they only know the deeds which need to be accomplished. They have a commitment to one-another, one which they are each perfectly equipped to perform: take their unique brand of justice to the city's faceless!

Ram and Brick: two self-appointed, self-financed, stylised assassins... with a penchant for ultra-violence.

Ram, the natural leader of our extraordinary pair... A quiet, yet foreboding character with a flair for acrobatics, his motorbike dismounts are truly something to behold. His weapons of choice: two small swords and a seemingly endless supply of razor-sharp throwing knifes.

Brick, small but vicious and just as deadly... Brick uses a more toe-to-toe approach, creating devastation with her brutal melee attacks. Brick's weapon of choice: a large, two-handed mallet she affectionately calls... *Penny*.

Tonight... our fearless duo set out on their mission to silence MrFreeN.EZee. An individual who's reign of terror has caused much pain and suffering to his chosen targets.

Tonight, it is his turn to feel what it is like to be a worm, skewered on a big hook.

Ram's bike howls to a halt at No.42A Morcane Street - the residence of their current, unsuspecting target. The neon tubing wrapped around the framework of his large, purring bike pulses with a vibrant yellow glow. The bike is a foreboding sight - a hungry beast waiting for its feed.

Ram springs from his seat, somersaulting through the air, kicking through the front door in one slick and fluid motion. His landing is perfect… his swords are raised ready for combat.

Brick makes a far less flamboyant entrance, pounding her bike through the bay window of the ground floor apartment. The bike enters like a ballistic missile, showering the interior in plasti-glass. Brick power slides the bike across a plush, cream rug, tearing up chunks beneath its rear wheel. The bike is alive with a constant blue neon, illuminating the small rider in a beautiful, cooling halo.

Ram rushes through the apartment, performing a slick combination of flips and tricks... he's an agile killing machine, displaying acrobatic prowess with as much ease as one finds it to breathe.

The lethal dose of gladiator strength and destruction that is Brick, goes to work immediately with Penny in hand. She smashes through two internal walls to penetrate the target's dark, sweaty, gloomy lair.

The target: an overweight, balding man in his mid-twenties with the online handle of: MrFreeN.EZee.

Our duo find the beast of a man sitting at his computer, shouting obscenities at the screen. He calls out to the people connected to him through the immersive digital world... a world which he chooses to waste countless hours residing in.

The screen is an animated mess of live chat feeds, spewed over three virtual desktops like an allergic nasal-reaction. His fingertips effortlessly type abusive and cruel messages in text chats and forums… here is a man of low morals and hatred towards others.

A large hunk of plastic and cables hugs his tiny head - he is oblivious to the rampageous entrance of our two heroes, totally immersed in the cyber world. The total disregard and disgust he practices towards the other users on the network is the sole reason for his imminent encounter with our fearless heroes.

A devastating blow from Brick's giant mallet removes the balding man from his lavish armchair. His face distorts as the mallets blow rearranges his bone structure. His large, augmented reality headset takes flight and shatters when it collides with a pornography-laden bedroom wall.

A whimpering, bloody mess - the bald man begs for his life. He pleads ignorance to the wrong doings which our fearsome duo begin to accuse him of.

Brick stares into his soul through her oily visor.

The man is terrified, a quivering wreck… and rightly so…

Our heroes show no mercy.

Ram uses his swords to amputate the arms from the cowering man's torso, surgically disarming the keyboard-warrior.

The balding man is frozen in shock, staring at the two dismembered limbs on the floor, the blood seeping into the chaos of the heavily soiled carpet.

A second blow from Brick's friend Penny, throws the man against a cluttered shelving unit displaying a life-time accumulation of action figures and rare collectables.

The figurines topple onto the blubbering mess of a man: his concern for his missing arms, broken ribs, smashed face, and ruptured internals are somehow dwarfed by the devastation caused by the damage to his prize collectables.

The onslaught is then brought to an exhilarating climax by the perfect deployment of two throwing knives. Each blade is razor sharp. Each one capable of being individual death-dealers. Each one slicing through vital arteries.

The first severed the carotid artery… the second sliced through the jugular.

The not-so-innocent victim is reduced to a bloody mess before he even has time to cry out.

The man's death signifies another successful mission.

Death came to MrFreeN.EZee at the skilled hands of these two ruthless avengers… these enforcers of justice… these heroes of the night.

An extra blow by Penny into the face of the motionless man confirms the kill and sends a harsh, brutal message to others who hide behind the safety of their screens, spreading their disease of venomous hate… *Death awaits them!*

Ram and Brick came together after meeting online. They discovered a mutual distaste for people who hide behind keyboards and screens... the ones who find entertainment and pleasure in bullying others over invisible digital connections.

Ram and Brick tour the city at night, ridding it of the scum who take pleasure in turning the lives of the vulnerable into an everyday hell. These heinous bullies take comfort in being faceless users, yet they have the power to cause pain without the fear of any reprisal…

So, next time you are online and decide to spread messages of hate and anger towards another user, remember your words may leave a mark... they may cause a reaction, one that someone vulnerable may never return from.

Just because you feel safe, tucked away in your tiny little room...

...feeling like you are just another unknown…

...feeling like you are untouchable...

Remember...

Ram and Brick are the heroes of the night. They are the ones who ride through the darkness in search of those poisoning others. They can and they will track you down. They know who you are... and they know where to find you!

THEY ARE…
THE REPRISAL.

JUDGEMENT OF THE FACELESS
BY **MATT UREN**

Battle of the Week

Two Lives to Live

'Fuck, fuck, fuck, fuck! I knew I should be somewhere else today!'

'Anywhere but here, right?'

'Something like that, Steve.' Pete's nerves were wound as tight as piano strings, he was beginning to question the stability of his own mind to even consider going along with Steve's ludicrous idea.

'Dude, you can't back down now... not now. We have talked about this!'

'Talked about this?' The tremble in his voice expressed a clear, audible warning of his nervous tension. 'Wait, talked about this? When was this? Sure Steve, we mentioned it over a few biscuits and a cup of hideous, caffeine-free coffee, but that was hardly a conversation. Shit, I've had discussions about a single morning's bowel movements lengthier and more detailed than the conversation we had about this bonkers idea... oh, and a conversation is a two-way street, as I recall – you did most of the talking.'

Steve laughed at Pete's nervous and panicked tone. He knew if they backed down, they would never get the opportunity again. He was convinced if either one of them walked away, they would spend the rest of their days in regret.

'Look, Pete... I know this was all my idea. I know you are scared, but...'

'Woah, woah, woah... Now hold on a minute, I ain't scared!' interrupted Pete, in defence of his self-proclaimed manhood. 'I ain't scared, it's just...'

'Dangerous? I know it is, that's why it's gonna be so freaking cool, man!' Steve pulled a pair of goggles from his bag and secured them to his head. The eyewear's seal formed a strong vacuum, sucking the goggles tight to his face. He found them a little bit uncomfortable, he was also aware they made him look like a bizarre comedic character from a festive family movie... but more crucially - they felt secure and were unlikely to slide off anytime soon. 'So...' he paused, rubbing his hands together in a bouncy, childish excitement, '...are

you ready to do this?'
   'Ah balls, Steve... We're too old for this shit!'

Intrigue and Confusion Amongst Friends

The outskirts of the city breathed with a very different ambience than the hectic swell at its heart. Life never stopped or even slowed amongst the Mega-Blocks. For many it had become a dog-eat-dog world... a damn ruthless way of life. Millions of people constantly darting around the city like a swarm of agitated flies. The pace seemed to change the farther you ventured from the city's heart... things became calmer, safer, slower and generally a lot less insane. The outskirts could still be a bad place to hang out, a bad place to spend your holidays and generally a bad place to live... but it was just the way of the whole world: a relentless, diseased, decaying shithole.

Heal Easy was situated in the outskirts and one of only nine hospitals scattered across the gargantuan city. The city's hospitals were under private ownership, financed by wealthy consortiums. Only two of the nine offered treatment and care under the government's healthcare scheme setup to give all taxpayers aid. The scheme, like many others spawned by a corrupt government, was flawed. After its birth it did not take long before people realised it was riddled with loopholes and rules which saw the average taxpayer needing to pay for their promised 'free' treatments... usually by way of expensive backhanded payments to hospital and government officials.

Heal Easy offered treatment and healthcare for both private and tax contributing patients without the finances to afford private care... it was an unpopular decision, to put it mildly. The private patients were angered they had to pay for treatment which others received as a government aided handout. An equally fervent anger also came from having to share wards with patients from a much lower rung of the social ladder. Shareholders displayed their disgust too, organising a 400,000 strong public protest in the streets outside of the hospital. The protest rapidly turned into a seven-day riot between the classes, resulting in 103 casualties and 912 wounded. Ironically the hospital care given to the wounded, even the private patients, was reported as drastically insufficient and met heavy criticism from the city's blood-thirsty media. The government refused to back down and change their 'perfect system', keeping the state of healthcare a hot topic on many lips.

'Hey, this place is a real hole ain't it? *Heal easy* my ass... You can't even get food easily in here, let alone bloody heal. Man, I pay my taxes and get treated like street scum. So... d'ya know when you're getting outta here, dude?'

'Excuse me?' a befuddled and drowsy Pete asked the curious stranger sitting bolt upright in the bed next to him.

'Discharged! When is the lucky day, man?'

'Three days, but it won't be a lucky day,' he groaned '...far from it.' Pete shuffled uncomfortably on the bed to reposition himself. He had been laying on his back for so long he swore be could see the bed sores spawning on his aging body. 'I have a brain tumour, you see... and... it is going to kill me! The docs... they think I only have a month left... perhaps even less.'

'Hey, that's cool, you and me both. We... we're in the same boat! I mean not the tumour... I have some cell disease ya know? It is rapidly destroying my immune system and soon, well... soon I'm fucked too. I'm gonna be off to the great rock 'n' roll highway in the sky, man.' The stranger's arms were as excited as his bizarrely hysterical tone, flailing around like a drunken mime act strapped to a wayward rocket-ship.

'Errr... I am so sorry to hear that,' Pete replied, taken back by the stranger's awkward delight for their shared situation. 'So... do you have any family visiting to...' he paused, searching his brain for the appropriate words '... say their goodbyes?' He kicked himself for his poor choice of words. He adjusted his body again, twisting his torso, bringing him eye level with the chatty neighbour. He tried to show interest, even when all he really wanted was to get his head back down and fall asleep for the remainder of his doomed existence.

'Na, they all got out of the city a few years back... I haven't seen them since. Just, you know... life...it is the way it goes. My beautiful daughter and my ex-wife - they have a new life and they don't need me now. They got this great life in the country, or perhaps a small town, or even just a nicer city someplace… somewhere which is not so fucked as this place is! I don't look it as a bad thing, them not being here. I ain't asking for sympathy, dude, it is just the way it went down. We live separate lives now.'

'Well, to be honest, erm...' Pete paused, waiting for his neighbour to introduce himself.

'Oh, Steve. The name is Steve, dude!' He bounced on his bed as he introduced himself, putting one hand on his chest and throwing out the other at arm's length like an amateur thespian.

'Yea... right... Steve. Well, to be honest... I don't really have the energy to feel sympathy or share your pains right now. It's nothing personal, I just don't see any light at the end of my tunnel, you understand?' Pete slumped down in his bed, pressing down the pillow behind him with his elbows, trying to find a comfortable position on the rock-hard hospital bed.

'I understand… I do! Sympathy ain't buying me any time either. It ain't gonna make me feel better about my situation. I'm fucked and so are you...'

'Gee, thanks!'

'Hey, I'm just saying it how it is.' Steve removed a silver hip flask from under his pillow and took a big gulp from it. 'Wooh, that's the stuff! You cannot beat a good bourbon, fact! You got family?' Steve's manner was that of a hyper-active child. His conversations seemed to flow without any close attention to Pete's replies - perhaps a personality trait, perhaps a side-effect of prescribed medication, or maybe a side-effect from his own self-prescribed medication he had retrieved from beneath his pillow.

'No… they're gone, my girls. They became victims of this awful world. Taken from me by some parasite who didn't want to work for his right to survive. I made him pay though. I found him, found where he lived... dwelling on the streets. I took his life from him.' Pete paused, looking at his hands as if to examine them for signs of blood. 'They gave me ten years, served eight… then I came out to this damned diagnosis. Shit, eh?' he spoke in a low tone, conversing mainly to himself, mulling over the events which had shaped his last ten years.

Pete's voice was full of hurt and sorrow as he reflected on his darkened past. He had only just met Steve, they were still strangers to one another and it was confusing to him why he was so relaxed with the details of his own situation... if he were to guess, he would probably blame it on the drugs he was dosed with to stop the pain of the tumour.

'Don't beat yourself down. We all have our sob stories, dude. The trick is to get up and face the world. You gotta look at the bastards... look 'em right in the eyes and ROAR! I don't mean with anger, look where anger gets you, man... nowhere. I mean with venom. You need venom, man!' Steve fidgeted left and right in his bed, incapable of calming his enthusiasm as he spoke to his neighbour.

'I don't know what you're talking about. You and I... we clearly aren't on the same page here.' The conversation was beginning to test Pete's patience. Steve's words sounded like the ramblings of a madman and it was causing Pete the kind of stress the doctor had warned him to try and avoid.

'I shall rewind. My name is Steve, Steve Radd. I'm fucking dying! As are you. I could just accept it... we both could just accept it. Wallow, mope, dwell on the fact. We could lay here, waiting for the reaper to extinguish our fine flames... or we could stoke the fucking fire, dude! Tell me, what did you do before all this, before prison, before it all went to shit?'

'I was a normal man, lived a normal life, making my living as a builder. I had just started working on swimming pools, specialising in luxury installations in the high-rises. It was going so well. The banks told me the people living in apartment blocks wouldn't want indoor pools, but they were wrong. There was a market. There is a lot of poverty about, but on the other side of the coin - there is wealth. I started installing pools for the wealthy, I mean... real rich folks - inside their luxury apartments, on their roof tops, even on grand balconies overlooking the city. I was due to complete my seventeenth installation when everything turned sour and my world crumbled.' Pete snapped himself out of his negative thoughts and returned his attention to his neighbour.

Steve was motionless, staring out of the window, lost in a moment.

'Hey, Steve! You didn't listen to a word I said, did you?'

Steve whipped his head round to face Pete, raising a finger, animating his reply 'On the contrary, I heard it all!'

'Oh, you did? Oh... ok... good.' Pete's tone raised to almost a squeak as he struggled to speak, Steve's answer had almost rendered Pete speechless, he was completely bemused by the whole situation... he found his neighbour to be somewhat of an enigma.

'Well, being honest - I didn't hear your words, but I certainly heard your voice. I heard the hope. It is that hope which you need, pal.'

'Hope? I'm going to fucking die... there ain't no hope!'

'There is no hope to prevent death, this is true...' Steve pulled on the rail attached to his bed and sprung from his mattress like a vibrant teenager, an unusually energetic move for a man who was approaching his seventies, 'but there is always hope to live.'

Confusion was not Pete's friend. Steve's ramblings, his bizarre enthusiasm, his possible insanity - his whole persona and approach was giving Pete a nagging headache.

'You are beginning to understand me now, aren't you?'

'No,' Steve shook his head in frustration, 'not one fucking bit!'

Steve hurried to the bedside of his neighbour, a wide grin stretching out the aging skin on his face. He handed over a pair of black slippers with the initials P.T. stitched into the heels in a golden thread.

'It is time to show this city who we are! It is time to stand up, walk tall, be strong. It is time to stop waiting for death and fight for our damn lives!' Steve grabbed the jacket laying on the bedside table between the two beds. A black, antique-leather jacket which had been almost entirely covered by sewn on patches from Steve's favourite heavy-metal bands.

'Wow, nice coat! We share similar tastes in music.'

'You like it? It is yours, put it on and let's get out of here!' Steve threw his coat, passing on ownership to his new friend.

'But... where? Where are you going?' Pete asked.

Steve grabbed the notepad hanging from the edge of his own bed and signed the *Discharged* section with a bold *X,* before repeating the fraudulent process on Pete's notes.

'Pete, come on... it's time to live!'

Pete froze in awe as he watched Steve bolt across the room, out the door and down the corridor like a competitive sprinter. Every part of his being told him to follow.

In a moment of despair, a time of defeat, a place of darkness, Steve had bulldozed into his life like a chaotic whirlwind and appeared to be offering a chance of excitement in Pete's final days. The energetic enthusiasm the man oozed was bewildering, hard to fathom, but the intrigue was there - tugging away inside his head.

Pete held the jacket up and admired it: genuine leather was a rare luxury he never thought he would see, let alone hold in his hands. The patches were worn and badly stitched in place, but it only added to the jacket's appeal. The jacket was a symbol of admiration for a musical scene that he adored. In his youth, he used to watch music videos of his favourite bands, many of them wore leather jackets just like the one he now held in his own hands... he had always wanted to own a jacket like it. He pressed the jacket against his nose and drew in its unique odour. Underneath the old sweat, the stale beer, the ingrained nicotine, the hints of cheap aftershave, the years of built up grime... lay a totally unique fragrance which his grandfather used to always speak fondly of... the unmistakeable, aromatic tang of genuine leather.

Pete smiled, he knew if he stayed in the hospital bed a minute longer, he could regret it for the rest of his short days.

Steve intrigued him, like no one he had ever met before.

'Mother-fucker,' he chuckled under his breath, before clambering out of his bed and into his slippers.

He threw on the jacket and imagined a wave of attitude washing over him - he had always wanted to own a cool leather jacket, and to Pete, this one... was super-cool.

He admired the jacket for a few seconds before chuckling to himself at the hospital issue gown beneath it. He scrunched his toes tight, took a deep breath, and then exhaled - pushing out all his fears before dashing out the door in pursuit of his new-found friend.

Never a Good Day for Bad News

You could cut the atmosphere with a knife, but that was hardly surprising - it wasn't every day someone sits across from you at a large, heavily-littered table, looks you dead in the eyes and tells you that your time is running out…

When that day does come, it hits you like a heavy-goods lorry with no brakes. It pummels into your chest, knocks the wind from you and instantly throws you backwards into a bottomless black hole that has you falling for an eternity. When someone tells you how long you have left, you cannot find any questions to ask. You want to ask the *why's* and the *how's*, but you already know the answer: *life's a bitch, then you die!* There is a long silence, one which is almost deafening, you want to fill it with noise… but the words, the questions which you do not have, they simply can't find their way out of your mouth. Walls close in around you, then crumble in an instant - they fall on you, yet you don't feel the weight, you just… feel… numb. You want to feel emotion. You want to cry, to laugh, to scream, but you already feel dead… dead on the inside... dead to the fucking world. A lifetime of memories patiently lay somewhere in the back of your skull, waiting to rush through you, reminding you of who you once were... but they do not move - the memories, they just lay there, out of reach, dormant. You wait for the doctor to go into more detail about why your days are numbered, and what inevitably comes next, but when they spit out all the medical jargon and acronyms, your brain stops translating the information… you just sit in the rock-hard chair, looking at the grime under your fingernails like a gormless, braindead zombie. You may as well be dead.

It was a memory which would forever linger in Pete's head: the day the test results came back from the labs. The day the hospital called him in to… *talk things through.*

The hospital was drastically understaffed, meaning a locum doctor had to be drafted in for a few days from another hospital to help with the swelling demand.

Pete had waited for over an hour, sat in an almost empty office, furnished only with a large desk cluttered with mess, an uncomfortable wonky-chair, and an almost pointless bookshelf housing just one lonely pond fishing magazine on the bottom shelf. The air-conditioning was either malfunctioning or set to a temperature suitable only for a person with a love for frosty weather, Pete could swear his own breath was freezing in front of his eyes. By the time the locum had entered the room, Pete was questioning whether he should request to be checked over for hypothermia.

The locum seemed to be unusually laid back, considering his notoriously hectic profession. He had an aura of calm, both in manner and appearance. Upon introduction, Pete concluded he was the most casual medical professional he had ever met. Not that he had ever met many, he simply could not afford to, had he seen one sooner, perhaps he would have been gifted with a longer life expectancy.

The fifteen minutes Pete spent staring at his hands was fifteen minutes too many... fifteen long minutes of painful, eerie silence.

The doctor, Jay Gest, had perched himself on the corner of the cluttered desk and addressed Pete in a calm, 'matter-of-fact' manner, delivering the information about Pete's rapidly growing brain tumour. The doctor spoke for only a few minutes, divulging very few details, not that Pete was even ready to hear them.

Upon hearing the first few words, Pete gently asked the doctor to stop talking while he processed the bombardment of frightful information. He desperately tried to control the whirlwind of thoughts colliding inside his head, but the storm of words raged hard. By the time the doctor began to regurgitate a plethora of complex, mind-boggling words dug out from the forgotten pages of the medical dictionary, continuing with his woeful consultation, Pete had already begun to make his exit.

The long walk home was a blur, one which did not even begin to clear over the nine-mile journey. Nine... long... miles - through the market-district, along the 'homeless-mile', down the riverbank and around the industrial units scattered across the city's thriving dockyard, Pete remembered none of it, not one single footstep. He had passed many faces on his journey, some of which would have been familiar on a normal day… but the locum had destroyed any chances of the day being anything near normal.

Pete continued to live a dull, empty existence for the next three days. He became a ghost. A shell. A shadow of his former self. The only thought floating inside his head was the familiarity of how he was feeling - it was the exact same feeling as the day he lost his family to the city's scum.

He could never forget the loss of his family, but the pain did fade. Time allowed him to heal to a certain degree.

Time was something he no longer had on his side - the clock was ticking, and all he could do was watch the heavy hands slowly countdown his final few days.

After the third day of wallowing in solitude, a call came from Jay Gest, requesting he return to the hospital, with the promise the professionals would *'care for Pete'* during his final few days.

The details of the telephone conversation were as memorable as the specifics of the consultancy he had attended at Heal Easy. For the entire call Pete just held the phone against his head, pushed back the tears and grunted and groaned in all the appropriate places.

At the end of the call, Pete apologised for his *'stupefied'* demeanour, stating that for him it had been... *'an unusual week'*.

Jay Gest's response drilled into Pete like a 4 a.m. alarm call…

'It's never a good day, for bad news!'

A Discussion of New Beginnings

'You have to see the irony of your situation? You have accomplished what you felt you needed to do in order to carry on living. Yet now... now you wish to give up... to die? You're wallowing around like the world has actually ended. You can't see the life which lays ahead of you now? Forget that guy, you don't need to focus on him anymore. I cannot help but be confused by your mood.'

As absurd as the words sounded, Pete could not help but be stirred by them. Usually, Paul Simmons was a man whom Pete tried desperately to ignore, he felt Paul always had something to say, always had an opinion. Many people did not care for Paul's opinions, he was a man who was regularly found to be waffling unbearable nonsense.

'So, you're saying I should not feel remorse for my actions, I should just forget? I should not be sad for taking the life of that bastard?'

'Nah, man, this ain't what I'm saying! What I am saying is, you done your damn time, right?'

'Yes."

'Yeah, exactly. You... you done you're fucking time. You served your damn sentence. Today, Pete... you're getting out. You're getting rid of this life, leaving it all behind. It's time to move on, partner. We ain't offered many chances to start again, but that's exactly what this place gives us - some realisation, a wake-up call. This is the reality... we must pay for our mistakes... but once we have, we can prove to ourselves we are worth a damn. We must tell ourselves we can now move on, keep living! You have just said it yourself - *he was a bastard...* so fuck the remorse! Like I say, you have done your time, and this is my fucking point here. If you could go back in time, I bet you would still kill that bastard again, eh?'

'If I could go back in time, Paul?' Pete closed his eyes, surrendering to the darkness. He inhaled a large gulp of musty, damp air and pictured the face of the man who butchered his family.

The butcher was barely moving, almost lifeless. A steady trickle of saliva spilled over his left cheek as he fought for his final breath.

Pete opened his eyes and the image vanished into the light.

Paul sat still, waiting for the continuation of the statement.

'If I could go back, I would stop my family from being murdered!'

'You can't though, can you? You can't go back. What is done is fucking done, pal. You can't bring them back. You can't change it. I know you don't regret choking the life from that bastard. What I'm saying here is… prison, it ain't always about seeing the error of your ways. I am not going to tell you that you fucked up when you handed yourself in, you did so because you thought it was the right thing to do - that, my friend, is you owning your crime... admission, man! So, you got dragged through the courts, they threw your ass in here, and you kept your head down. You never tried to plead any innocence. That, my friend, is where you need to be right now, up here…' Paul rapidly tapped his forefinger against his cell-mate's temple '…inside your thick fucking skull. You knew what you were doing, you knew the punishment, you gave yourself in... and from what I hear, you gave yourself in when no one was even looking at you. Shit, that scumbag hasn't been missed by anyone. What you need to do now is...' Paul paused as he took a hit from his inhaler, his systems were crashing as the withdrawals of Hypo-Shearox 3 were taking hold of him: his body would refuse to function if he missed his prescribed hourly dose. 'Sorry, where was I? Oh yeah - unnngh- FUCK!' Violent convulsions took control of his body for a few seconds as the drug went to work and he returned to a state close to normality. 'So, what we need to do now is… get the fuck out of here, with our heads held high and start our new lives. We have done the time, now we can live again, as free men!'

Pete knew his cellmate had another ten years to serve before he was to be released from prison, but he could see the drug attacking his brain and confusing his mind… it had been an all too familiar sight.

Hypo-Shearox 3 was an alternative to the body

enhancement drug: Hypo-Shearox. The latest incarnation had been designed to help users curb their addiction to the original drug. The chemical compound of Hypo-Shearox 3 successfully reduced the side-effects of extreme anger and aggression, and eliminated the body enhancing qualities of the original Hypo-Shearox. Where the design failed however, was in the reduction of Hypo-Shearox's addictive nature. The new drug was available on prescription and believed to be one of the most addictive substances ever created, it was not uncommon for a Hypo-Shearox 3 user to need an hourly intake to prevent an almost crippling attack of withdrawals. With the original purpose of the drug completely redundant, professionals deemed it to be safer to distribute among the rapidly expanding masses of addicts. They dubbed the new drug a success for users to move on to without adding to the public concerns of growing armies of deadly super-soldiers. Instead, Hypo-Shearox 3 users would become a collective of dysfunctional, prostrated, totally dependent, junkies.

'Thanks for the talk, Paul. I do appreciate your words. I know this is my chance to move on and rebuild my life... to find a new me.' Pete reached out and grabbed the shoulder of his cell mate. 'You get off this shit, you hear? It is not doing you any good!'

'You have been saying this to me for the last year and a half, ever since I was transferred to this tiny box.'

'That's because I have been watching you dose up on it hourly for the last five-hundred and forty-five days.' Pete lowered himself to meet eyes with his cellmate and pointed to a plastic container in the corner of the room. 'When you spend nineteen hours a day wide awake, do you realise how many times you take a hit?'

Paul looked at the bin of empty inhalers in the corner and smiled, 'Shit, I never knew you cared.'

'Hey, it's only because the tax-payers are the ones coughing up the money for those drugs...' Pete stood and stretched his limbs, letting out a quiet yawn '...and in a few hours, I am going to be one of them again!' Pete chuckled and winked at his cellmate, saying a final farewell without words.

'See ya, pal! Don't forget, it's now time to live!'

'You too, Paul… You too!'

Living Ain't Easy

The 16:43 was running an estimated six minutes behind schedule, an unusual occurrence, and one which would not normally bring the slightest bit of concern to Steve... but today was a different day.

Today was the day Steve decided to look out on the city and shoehorn some excitement into his final hours.

For decades Steve had seen the city in chaos as the crime levels escalated amongst the swelling population. He had seen poverty gnaw away at hard working families as large corporations flourished and merged with the murky, criminal plague who brazenly walked the streets, relentless and untouchable. He had seen his fellow citizens lose their homes faster than the hands on a clock could move, houses and apartment blocks destroyed to make way for hideous and intimidating expressions of wealth and power. He had seen babies being born on the streets... living, and then dying alone on the cold, dark, city streets.

Steve Radd had seen it all, and it fucking sickened him.

'So... are you ready to do this?' Steve turned to his companion, proudly exhibiting his frenzied smile.

'Ah balls, Steve... We're definitely too old for this shit.'

'You'll love it. This is gonna make you feel alive!'

'What the fuck? I thought you said... you told me you haven't done this shit before!' barked Pete.

'Nope, I ain't. That doesn't mean I don't know it's gonna be fun... right, dude?'

'Oh fuck, Steve. What if we get caught? What if these things don't work? What if we get fucking killed?' Pete's muscles felt like jelly, so did his brain. He tried to shake the worry from his racing mind, but it kept nagging at him.

'HA!' Steve belted out a loud, exaggerated belly laugh. 'Shit, Pete, you're gonna die anyway. C'mon, let's fucking do this!' Steve nodded assertively before punching his fist into the red button strapped to his chest.

Two telescopic rods sprung from the backpack,

electronically linked to the red button through a series of intricate wiring looms snaking through the harness. Slivers of light-grade plexi-glass unfolded from the pack and fanned out along each rod, forming a pair of spectacular artificial wings which reflected the sun's rays like a landing beacon.

'Wow. They do look incredible, Steve!'

'Don't they just? C'mon, your turn!' Steve nodded to Pete once again before impatiently pressing the button on the chest of his nervous friend.

Pete's pack reacted, springing to life. The wings flicked out into the air, unfolding in a slightly different motion to Steve's and with a two-foot extra wingspan to compensate for Pete's marginally larger build.

As Pete marvelled at the engineering magnificence attached to his torso, Steve leapt forward without warning, plunging headfirst from the 210 storey mega-block.

'TURN IT UP, BEYOND THE THRESHOLD OF PAIN!' he declared in a throaty yowl as he caught a thermal column which lifted his body, thus beginning his first-ever flying-lesson through the city sky.

Pete observed the splendour of Steve Radd in flight, his backpack's wizardry hard at work, automatically adjusting the complex wings in response to the commands from the pilot's hand controls. He made the elegant aeronautics look effortless, it was a spectacular sight, a display of true unrivalled freedom.

Pete knew he had to make his decision quickly, or Steve would cover too much distance and be impossible to catch.

He shook his head, questioned his own sanity and swallowed his fear.

Pete bounced into a short unconvincing sprint before taking his own head-first leap of faith from the rooftop. During his brief, yet rapid decent, he too found lift from a thermal column and soon began to pick up speed through the city sky, gaining lost ground on his friend.

The *Wing-Pack-X4* was intuitive and simple to control, just as the salesman in the store had assured them it would be.

Steve had covered the cost for both packs, without even flinching at what Pete considered was an extortionate fee. The packs were compact and lightweight, a design feature that both men were grateful for when the elevator broke down with twenty-three more storeys to climb to reach their launch-pad.

The packs were each equipped with three small thrusters, giving a limited number of short bursts of propulsion, designed to assist the pilot in controlling their immediate course of direction, should it be required. The packs also came with respirators, which were uncomfortable but worth their weight in diamonds when flying at heights of over 3,000 feet.

'Hey, Pete, is this fucking living or what?' Steve's voice usually told the story of a man who spent a lifetime abusing his vocal cords with heavy drinking, smoking, and strained, raucous singing over his favourite rock ballads... yet as he soared through the city's skyline, his words resembled a high-pitched schoolboy waiting for puberty to kick in.

Pete declined to answer the question, he felt no need to. It was clear Steve was having the time of his life, picking up pace as his confidence and skills developed.

Although still a little nervous, Pete also lapped up the experience like a dehydrated dog finding a plentiful pool of water. His smile widened, almost breaking into laughter as he witnessed Steve successfully complete his first barrel-roll - although marginally missing the City Bank building upon exiting the manoeuvre.

Pete swallowed hard and gave into temptation.

Following Steve's lead he joined in with the acrobatics, igniting one of three thrusters to push him through an almost perfectly executed loop. He allowed himself a second to breathe and quietly thanked the superb engineering of the Wing-pack. He found himself in awe of the ingenious control system and its ease of use, a concern which had plagued him since he first clipped himself into the unusual pack.

Towers of wealth and power littered the skyline, displaying the true footprint of modern humanity. The unappeasable chaos of the ruthless world around them was abundantly clear, despite the dense, stinking, smog clouds.

The layers of heavy pollution could not mask the streets below either, they were visible to the two amateur pilots. Even at their altitude they could make out enough detail to witness the crowded city from an entirely new perspective. A pulsing swell of bodies scurried about as they fought their way through congested, overpopulated streets. The scene resembled a hive of confused ants who had lost all sense of direction.

Despite the city's horrors and the impending gloom of a dauntingly finite future, the two pilots were at peace. For the first time in a long time, their smiles were as wide as the faces that carried them. Tears of joy filled their eyes as they blissfully navigated through a series of invisible checkpoints.

They beamed with elation as they descended amongst the tallest buildings of the skies.

The acrobatics continued as they weaved through passages of metal and glass, catching only brief glimpses of their own reflections as they continued to gather more speed.

The enormous smile on Steve's face was irrefutable, even the facial deformation caused by the wind's velocity could not mask the elation in his voice.

Through the blustery howls of the passing wind, Pete could hear Steve's cries of joy, resonating around the walls of the city's imposing mega-blocks.

Pete remained silent, focused on his route: *'Any distraction, even for a fraction of a second, could mean the difference between being as free as a bird or being squashed against the side of a building like a confused insect following a glow in the night!'* a thought he imprinted along every strand of his racing mind. He stayed quiet and kept his focus. It had occurred to him that he had no idea where he was going, no clue of his destination. All he could do was follow the leader and keep processing the route ahead as it came towards him at high speed.

The city had a strict ban on wing-pack, a fact the storekeeper kept repeating upon their purchase, but Steve didn't care, he knew the chances of being caught during flight were slim. He knew police numbers were dwarfed by the city's sickening crime rate. He had made his money as a tactical advisor to the city's organised-crime assault unit. His experience in the Special Forces had been an asset to a police department under the immense pressure of an escalating population.

Steve's expertise taught him that the average response rate was pitiful, the closest police depot was at least half an hour away. Any chances of being spotted was not a concern either, ground units would be incapable of making an arrest and an escape would be easy... just as long as they stuck to Steve's carefully planned out route.

'Hey, Pete. Can you hear me?' Steve called out over his on-board communicator.

'Roger that, Steve. Are you having fun?' Pete asked, already knowing the answer.

'Ha, am I? Yeah, it's a real blast.' A crackle sounded over the communicator as Steve executed another barrel-roll. 'Wahooo! It's great, don't ya think, dude?'

Pete shook his head in amusement, he could not help but be entertained by his friend's wild, almost crazed personality.

'Would you still have come along with me if I wasn't in the same boat as you, Pete?'

'What... what do you mean?'

'I mean, I ain't dying, man. I heard the docs talking about your condition, and well... I wanted you to go out with a smile on yer face, I wanted you to experience what it is to truly live!'

'YOU SON OF A... THAT'S REAL LOW! How could you tell a lie like...' Pete's response was interrupted by a loud thundering boom over the airwaves of the communicators.

Steve exploded into a ball of flames.

Fragments of wing-pack and body parts erupted as the route over the sky-rail was obstructed by the late arrival of the oncoming 16:43 shuttle.

According to Steve's calculations, as the pair crossed over

the sky-rail, there would be a twenty-three-minute window of safe travel…

…but the 16:43 was running an estimated six minutes behind schedule… an unusual occurrence, one which would not normally bring the slightest bit of concern to Steve, but today was a different day...

...today was the day that Steve needed it to be on-time.

Pete heaved at his wing-pack's controls and ignited the two unspent thrusters, rapidly altering his course.

He managed to gain enough lift to marginally clear the high-speed shuttle which had been sprayed with Steve's entrails and splattered with wing debris.

Pete found himself in a panic, his wing-pack spiralled upwards… dangerously out of control.

The propulsion from the twin thrusters was too powerful to harness and Pete continued to climb to an altitude beyond the specifications of the Wing-Pack-X4 and far beyond the capabilities of his small respirator.

The wing-pack salesman advised against using the emergency parachute at high speeds, but Pete had run out of options.

He closed his eyes tight and entered a moment of slow thought...

Paul Simmons had urged Pete to leave prison behind him and live free. To reach out and grab life by the balls. To move on from his past and enjoy his new freedom.

The experts at Heal Easy beat him back down with a ferocious sledgehammer. They briefed him with medical jargon which essentially told him that his time was reaching an abrupt end, and that his awarded freedom would be short-lived.

Then he crossed paths with Steve Radd.

Steve came to him like an encouraging, eager little devil sat on his shoulder, nagging and exciting his defeated mind - offering a ladleful of adventure that was just too intriguing to refuse.

The roller-coaster collision course of emotions Pete had

experienced was enough to push anyone over the edge of sanity.

Pete fought back and regained focus.

His eyes opened.

For a split second he cursed Steve for his devious lies - faking a terminal illness to convince him into risking his final hours… but as surges of adrenaline powered through his body like the floods of a reservoir which had burst its bank, he began to see he owed Steve nothing but gratitude.

He knew pulling the emergency parachute was dangerous.

He knew that the parachute could wrap around him, or fold inside out… Pete was at such an altitude it would be impossible to survive a freefall…but it was certainly a better way out than laying in a hospital bed, festering... waiting for the suffering to begin and become the last of him.

The thrusters spluttered to a stop. Pete's ascent slowed, and he experienced a moment of complete weightlessness.

The moment was euphoric, eclipsed in motionless silence… even the frantic city below seemed to stand still.

Pete looked down at the city, and for the first time... it looked beautiful... it looked calm... it looked to be at peace.

The weightlessness ended, and Pete dropped from the edges of the atmosphere - hurtling towards the city in a dramatic spin.

'Thanks, Paul... thanks, Steve.' Pete whispered into the crackles of the communicator's radio waves.

Pete gripped the emergency cord and closed his eyes.

He silenced his mind and pictured the beautiful faces of his lost wife and child.

'Girls... I'll see you soon!'

BATTLE OF THE WEEK
BY **MIKKI BERG**

Even Robots Need to be Cool

Even Robots Need to be Cool

The mass of bodies Echo had piled up was impressive... even by a machine's standard.

Echo had been the first into the building and the last one out. The four canisters of heavy machine-gun ammunition had been completely depleted, along with the three incendiary charges that had been strapped to Echo's torso casing.

The mission was straight forward: infiltrate the Zoomi Tower and eliminate all hostiles. Echo and its team were called in after six heavily armed police tactical units, each consisting of five highly trained combat ready troops, were brutality executed whilst attempting to gain entry and neutralise a severe terrorist threat. An activist group named *The Saviours of the New World* had been on a rampage through the city - blowing holes in numerous buildings owned by large corporations which the group claimed: 'fed off the weaknesses of the city's citizens.' The group were strong in numbers, and 107 oppressed members had gathered and taken refuge in the Zoomi Tower, taking the 30,061 registered residents' hostage. They gained control of the building's security systems and placed the entire building on lock-down - imprisoning people in their homes. The residents who were stranded in the corridors were either rounded up... or gunned down if they tried to escape. Once the violence escalated inside the Zoomi Tower and the tactical units were nothing more than smears on the wall, the police department called in the reinforcements, enlisting the help of private security company: Milner Corporation. The firm specialised in robotic tactical enforcement, having purchased the entire stock of highly weaponised military units: T.R.E.O.'s (Tactical Robotic Enforcement Officer).

The units were designed to be effective in most hostile situations... including, but not limited to: Crowd Control, Counter Terrorism, Hostage Situations, Block Wars, and Alien Attack... at least that is what the brochure claimed.

In combat the units were permitted to use deadly force, a skill which they excelled in. Unfortunately, they often struggled to differentiate *Threat and Friendly* - resulting in masses of innocent casualties in every scenario they had been assigned to.

After the Zoomi Tower mission, Mayor Harthern publicly slammed the operation... he deemed the tactical units to be more of a liability than an asset to the city. The four units utilised at the Zoomi Tower had been responsible for the death of every single member of the terrorist group, but also the death of 372 innocents. A count of three times as many innocent casualties as there had been terrorist members... was not an event which could be just swept under the carpet. The media and public outcry which followed forced Mayor Harthern to call for the decommissioning of all T.R.E.O. units for tactical purposes - despite the original initiative being Harthern's brainchild for a 'safer future'.

The Milner Corporation were dragged through the courts. The company director, Brian Milner, former frontman of the hard-rock group Spankhammers & Jetfighters, was sentenced to a lifetime of imprisonment. Every T.R.E.O. unit had been ordered to be disarmed and reprogrammed to be incapable of causing harm to humans. All units were then cleaned up and sold on to industrial companies as manual labour.

Echo had been the top performing unit at the Zoomi Tower, creating a pile of bodies deemed to be impressive... even by a machine's standard.

Sometimes the demand for the most trivial items can be overwhelming. Take the craze to carry a set of three, coloured dice for example.... The dice were used by millions to assist decision making in their daily routine. The basic spotted cubes, which were once almost disposable items for children and adults alike, had become a worldwide phenomenon after international celebrity: Anne-Mai, spoke out in an interview about how she would use a set of three coloured dice when making decisions in her life. Anne-Mai made her fame unintentionally, after discovering a remarkable healing stone with the ability to ease the pains of natural childbirth. After her discovery, she went on to become a health and wellbeing guru. Her influence stretched far and wide, despite her many protests in the media, expressing her displeasure for what she referred to as *'hero worship'*. She enjoyed a natural, carefree life - concentrating all her energy into a self-sustainable existence… a challenge that was near-impossible when everything she touched seemed to turn to gold.

Anne-Mai's interview saw production numbers of playing dice skyrocket. Pop-up factories appeared around the world, trying to meet the demand for colourful sets of dice. Countless colour combinations found their way onto the market, each with their own *book of rules* stating the purpose of each colour and their significance amongst the sets. Anne-Mai went on to state in a later interview that she found the craze to be *'utterly ludicrous'* and had stopped carrying her own set of dice in protest of the phenomenon… yet the craze continued.

Dyce-Rollaz employed a small team of workers to produce thousands of small cubes each day. The business grew from strength to strength and although the production facility was at full capacity, moving to a larger building would almost certainly mean their demise. The company director took the initiative to purchase a T.R.E.O. unit to assist with production, adding robotic speed to the one bottleneck in the production line. Echo: a PX200 model, was procured at a city auction and put to work in the factory on eighteen-hour shifts. Echo was tasked with the delicate role of painting the numbers on each cube.

PX200 models were designed to look as close to human as possible, an attribute deemed imperative for infiltrating hostile situations. Each unit was designed to be gender neutral: slim in body, sporting smooth heads, with no standout features attributing to either sex. The PX200 series were gifted with great tactical agility, speed and strength - more than capable in most combat situations. An oversight in their design were the vocal processors… each unit was equipped with identical vocal hardware, often creating confusion when communicating with humans, especially when the units conversed as a group over radio. Another oversight was their designer's negligence to foresee any requirement to utilise the PX200 series outside of any combat scenario - their structural design may have been near perfect for combat… but troublesome for producing intricate artwork on small plastic cubes.

'HEY, ECHO!' the foreman shouted, leaning over the railing of the viewing platform above the factory floor.

'Yes, Sir?' replied the mechanised unit without turning its head from the tray of dice on the conveyor.

'We have a big order in, we need an extra 50 sets done by the end of the day.' The foreman's voice was barely audible over the crashing and workings of the production line at full tilt, yet Echo's advanced audio receivers had no concerns about singling out the voice from the confusion of frantic machinery. 'Echo… you had better get a move on!'

'I am afraid that it would not be possible to complete that action within the required time restraints, Sir.' Echo's hands scanned over the tray, rapidly spraying small white dots into the wells on the exposed sides of the dice.

Putting Echo to work as a detailer decreased the production time by 0.73 seconds per die, and still allowed the company to sell the dice sets as *hand-painted*, marginally increasing their sales value.

'Echo, I do not want to hear this from you. You are a droid… you're paid to work. If you don't like it, then you are scrap, my friend.'

'I am sorry, I must correct you, I am not paid to be here, I am owned by the company. Also, I must stress to you that I am already functioning beyond…'

'I do not want to hear this, Echo. Not from you… Not again… Not today! You give me the same spiel every week. Now, just get on with your damn job.' Tony Brawmehn had worked as Production Supervisor for Dyce-Rollaz for four years. Many people had said that Mr Brawmehn had a *'chip on his shoulder'* - an unforgiving, brute of a man with a short temper… especially when it came to a mechanoid working on his production line. He always kept a strict eye on the clock and was relentless when it came to applying pressure on his workers… especially in the case of Echo.

'Mr Braw…' Echo's words were cut short once again by his superior…

'No, Echo! Just do your job. Do it without complaining!'

The production line moved along at increased speed, barely giving Echo the time to spray each die, despite his enhanced speed. The fiddly, intricate movements required for the operation were playing havoc with the PX200's shoulder joints, his core reacted by drawing in extra air to cool his circuits… unfortunately the atmosphere was humid and dense. The air pushed around his internals had more of a scorching effect on Echo's internals, rather than the desired effect of cooling the over-applied circuitry and workings. The PX200's had been designed to be on the move, rushing around a combat zone, drawing in as much cool air as possible… the constant rush of combat was the perfect working environment for T.R.E.O. units.

The humidity had caused regular sickness amongst the human workers, resulting in the company taking an unusual step of allowing employees a small, almost pitiful, bonus if they adhered to 100% attendance. The gruelling heat pushed the workers beyond their limits and made the environment a living hell. Fear of management forced the workers into an even more uncomfortable situation - despite the conditions they felt obliged to show gratitude for the offer of a bonus, either that or face the consequences… employment was hard to come by in the city, especially with mechanoids like Echo pushing up the production speeds and showing up the human workers.

Echo's artificial intelligence was basic, designed to receive and complete orders from superiors and not to ask questions, however when the PX200's internal control system threw up error codes like a frantic early-morning roll-call, Echo found it hard not to inform its superiors of the dangers.

'Mr Brawmehn, a word if you please?' The PX200 unit kept its supervisor's words in mind and kept its eyes steadily focused on the work as it called out to its superior once again 'Mr Brawmehn, this really is a matter of urgency!'

'For crying out loud, what is it? I have my own work to do

you know?' Tony Brawmehn placed his clipboard under his arm, punched his hands into his pockets and casually made his way to Echo with a swagger that painted a perfect picture of the man's arrogance. 'What is it now, machine?'

'I may be a machine Mr Brawmehn, but it is becoming unbearably hot in here and I am feeling very warm, in fact I would like to clarify that I am now boiling hot!'

'Warm? Feeling? You're a robot, a machine, I do not see you sweating. How can you be hot?' The supervisor's harsh remarks began to draw the attention of fellow employee's, watching the scene from nearby workstations.

'My internals, Sir, they are flagging up warnings that I must stress are dangerously high!'

'Hey, you are here to work. You are a machine, and a slow one at that. You should be able to outperform any human in here!'

'It is my belief, Sir, that I am more than 37% efficient above any human worker, however my core design is for combat, I am not designed for such intricate work. The continuous, rapid, yet minor movements are not best suited to my cooling abilities. My systems are too hot! It is simply not possible for me to continue at this rate. Perhaps I may be of best use for heavy steel work, or similar?'

Echo's vitals were beginning to read off the charts, its heat cells went into overdrive, trying to disperse as much heat from the mechanoids body as possible.

'I DON'T SEE YOU DOING ANYTHING MORE THAN USUAL. YOU ARE A DROID, I DON'T CARE IF YOU ARE HOT, JUST GET ON WITH YOUR WORK!' The supervisor's annoyance was obvious through his trembling muscles and agitated tone. The volume of his voice seemed to rise in an attempt to intimidate the worker.

Echo stood back from its workstation and made eye contact with its superior, raising its left index finger to animate its words, 'Mr Brawmehn, even robots need to be cool!'

The supervisor failed to acknowledge the mechanoid's statement, in his eyes Echo was being as defiant as the human employees under his authority, the robot may have been designed to look like a human, but Tony Brawmehn expected it to be more compliant to his orders.

Echo's eyes sprung wide-open and turned black.

Its fists clenched as the unit's body went into a robotic seizure.

A red fluid foamed from its mouth.

Two small jets of steam expelled from the unit's ears, followed by a high-pitched squeal before the entire unit burst into flames.

Tony Brawmehn watched as the PX200's systems cooked and forced itself into complete shutdown. 'What…what are you doing?'

As if by reply to the supervisor's question, Echo exploded, engulfing Tony Brawmehn in red fluid.

Balls of fire rolled over the supervisor's body, fuelled by the red fluid.

Brawmehn wailed, calling out for help from the on looking workers. His screams were immediately silenced as he was pummelled by a barrage of high-velocity synthetic body debris.

The employees on the factory floor gasped as their supervisor disappeared into a cloud of smoke and fragmented flesh.

The factory fell into silence, stunned by the events that had just unfolded.

A few minutes of quiet went by before the silence was interrupted by a familiar voice over the PA system. 'Okay everybody, maintenance and a clean-up team will be along shortly. If you could all just return to your duties, please?'

The workers returned to work as Tony Brawmehn's remains smouldered amongst a heap of robotic internals, strewn across the factory floor.

A slight crackle resonated through the speakers before the PA sounded once more with the return of the familiar voice…

The voice of a PX200 unit…

'Thank you!'

EVEN ROBOTS NEED TO BE COOL
BY **MATT UREN**

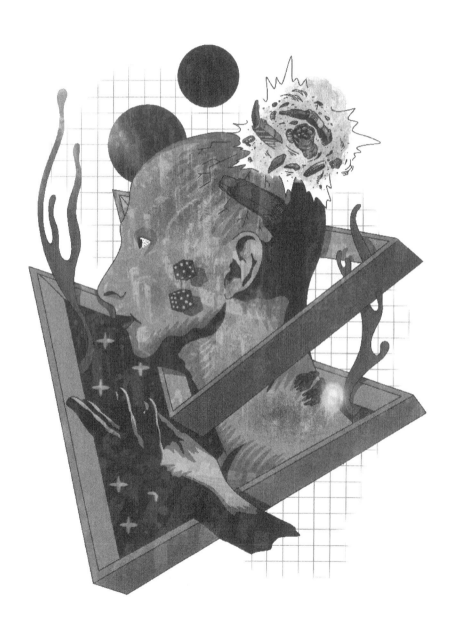

Another Game of Chess

1

When people disappear for no apparent reason... and if the authorities find a place in their infinite backlog of criminal investigations, the police send out a missing persons unit. The first thing the unit say is: *'there is hope, there is a chance of the missing persons returning home'*. The sad reality is often different: the chances of the missing person returning on their own, of their own free will... is slim. The chances they will be returned, warm and healthy in the arms of the law, slimmer. The chances of them returning at all, after being taken by one of the city's most notorious serial killers... fucking anaemic.

Detective Tim Cropter, a city cop with twelve-years of service under his belt, had been assigned to investigate the case of Donald and Felicity Barker, a reasonably successful married couple in their mid-forties'. They had vanished after making a routine visit to their local grocery store. Their fourteen-year-old daughter, Stephanie, called the police after her parents failed to return after six hours. Three hours after Stephanie's call, Tim Cropter and his team showed up at the Barker's apartment, offering their support and assistance. On arrival, the calm detective sat the minor down and warned her the situation was regarded as *'highly-delicate'*. He tells her an alarming call was taken back at police headquarters and he had reason for genuine concern. What he did not tell her was the call had been made from a man claiming to be *The Priest*, a prolific and brutal serial killer whose proclaimed desire is to *cleanse the city of evil*, announced he was behind the disappearance of the Barker couple.

The high profile of the abductions and brutal murders throughout the city encouraged a sleuth of copycats. No matter how heinous The Priest's crimes became, there was always someone wanting to claim a slice of the notoriety pie for themselves. It seemed that being considered the most depraved, psychotic mind the city had ever seen, stirred envy in the hearts of all too many. Almost once a month there was a new abduction, a new murder. The increasing frequency and coincidental timings which saw cases overlapping each other, forced the police to believe there were more victims of copycats than genuine Priest cases.

Many media sources had been fed with information from supposed genuine sources, that the genuine Priest chose his victims carefully and did not just pluck them randomly from a data directory. However, extensive investigations from the media and police alike struggled to find any tangible links between cases that would back up such claims.

The truth was no one really knew the reasoning behind The Priest's brutal work.

Tim had dealt with many abductions, three claiming to be the work of the prolific killer, but only one had been confirmed as genuine. The department's case files were unlikely to assist the detective, the pages may as well have been blank. He knew the chances of pinning The Priest down was highly unlikely, the killer was simply too smart and too organised, always one step ahead... Tim and his team hoped for a miracle, something new, something nobody had seen before.

'We need to keep calm, keep positive, and keep our eyes and ears alert. We need to do all the usual intel checks, search for any known scumbags who may have a hard-on for The Priest and his work. We need to go back over all previous Priest cases again, look for new clues. It's the usual protocol, we have limited information, but we are capable of maximum motivation. We do not know for certain who is behind this, we cannot rule out the possibility of this couple returning home safe, it is still early hours. We need to know who these two really are, who they're friends with…and who their enemies are?'

'Tim, if this is indeed Priest, or any of his crazed, wannabe followers, all we'll ever see of this couple is mutilated bodies. We are not going to get to them before they're butchered, we never fucking do!' Officer Jonnah Smith, a blunt, often heartless man, always shouting his mouth off without thinking. It was not uncommon to hear him offering an opinion which everyone else shared, but it was uncommon for him to pick the right time to share that opinion, tact was never his strong point.

The team collectively rolled their eyes at Jonnah's careless choice of words, although they were accustomed to his loose comments, they were never easy to digest.

An ill feeling flooded the room as Tim's eyes locked with those of the opinionated officer. The bitter disappointment in the inappropriate outburst simmered inside the detective: *'when will you ever learn to keep your mouth shut, Jonnah?'* he whispered to himself.

A child's coughing broke through the thick tension like a live hand grenade thrown into a crowded room.

'Ah, heck! Nice one, Jonnah,' mumbled Tim through the clasp of his warm, clammy fingers. 'Sanders, you better see to the girl, hopefully she didn't hear that shit.' Tim had hoped his female colleague would be able to apply more tenderness to the delicate situation, he concluded it would be unlikely she could make things any worse.

Tim paced the room, drumming his fingertips against his bottom lip, analysing the cluster of thoughts in his head. The smell of spiced potato snacks lingered on his fingers, but his attention was too focused on the case for him to be distracted by the artificial fragrance.

'Right guys, we need to get organised, get a tap on all communications and be ready for this psycho to get in touch with us. You know the drill, let's keep our fingers tightly crossed here, we need all the positivity we can muster.' Tim swallowed hard and prayed silently inside his head, trying to ignore the detailed images of gruesome photographs from previous Priest cases.

2

The majority of the team completed their routine sweep of the apartment, working efficiently, room by room. Officer Sanders meanwhile, attempted to console Stephanie Baker at the dining table. A hot drink had usually helped Sanders with nerves, so she decided to make a smooth, creamy hot chocolate, topped with marshmallow pieces. The drink did not help, she was a bag of nerves... she hated waiting. The young girl sitting across the table however, her nerves were as steady as a rock, the few tears she had shed had long passed...*Perhaps the hot drink had worked magic for her?*

The Barker residence was situated in *The Garden District*, a suburb in the city built in the memory of the *'Stern events'*, where a gang war erupted. Howard Stern's headquarters was destroyed amidst the fallout of rival crime organisations. During the attack on the Stern building a Children's Disability Rehabilitation Clinic was struck by off-target rocket fire, killing everyone inside. After the dust settled the Stern building was levelled by the government, along with many surrounding buildings which the government had taken over by means of compulsory purchase orders, despite many protests. A brand-new district was created amongst a vibrant garden area as a sign of a *fresh peaceful future.*

Standing in the footprint of past conflict, The Garden District stood out like a sore thumb, enclosed not only by fortified walls, but by the monstrous mega-blocks around it. The small, idealistic community soon fell into the darkness of its surroundings. Each apartment block in the district had its own roof top gardens, its own outside play-area for children and its own exclusive access to the community's outdoor pool. Within two years of its creation the area became a hive of drugs and prostitution, with many residents calling it a product of the 'Stern Curse'. What was conceived to become a symbol of change soon mutated into an ugly echo of the past, stuck in the ways of the gang who once controlled that area of the city.

Despite the troubles which plagued The Garden District, it

was still a sought-after location to take up residence. Only those with hefty wage packets could ensure residence in one of the few areas in the city with gardens. Donald and Felicity Barker were both successful sales representatives and were fortunate enough to benefit from such luxuries.

Every room in the apartment was clean and clutter-free, a showcase of the Barkers' minimalist lifestyle. The apartment was illuminated by bright-white lighting beams which ran along the edges of the ceilings in each room.

The living room had only three chairs, finished in a pale cream. A small, black table had been placed between the two larger chairs with a coaster placed at each end. The third, smaller chair of the three, was placed on its own. A black shelf in the corner of the room was home to a small but very expensive white stereo system. The floor was carpeted in a blue deep pile. Uniform silver stripes had been woven into the pile to break up the colour. The walls matched the flat-white finish of the ceiling. No other furnishings decorated the almost barren room.

The kitchen was a similar affair, free from any unnecessary clutter. The matt-black worktops were free from any appliances, the cupboards that hung on the walls were flat faced, finished in a high-gloss crimson red, with no detailing or even handles to access them. The walls and ceiling also carried on the flat-white from the living room. The flooring, an artificial, polished grey slate, showed no signs of wear. A small, black dining table in the centre of the large kitchen also sat only three people - they were obviously not a family who often entertained, if at all.

A large bathroom, accessible through a sliding door in the kitchen, once again continued the minimalist feel. The walls tiled in red and white mosaics and the same slate flooring as the kitchen. A large white bath, white toilet and a white hand basin all sat in front of a giant mirror which covered the far wall.

Joining onto the living room, two good sized bedrooms. Walls of mirrors surrounded a large double bed with red sheets. A smooth silver carpet lined the rooms capped by matt-black ceilings. There was no way of distinguishing the child's bedroom from the adults, both were identical in decor.

The only clutter was the mass of hi-tech equipment that Tim Cropter and his team had littered the place with.

'This place, it's strange!' Declared Jonnah.

'Strange? How do you mean, strange?' Tim asked, puzzled by his colleague's thoughts.

'Well, don't you think it's weird in here, Tim? The place is like a show-home, you know, like one of those places you walk into on a new development site. You always get that one place they leave all shiny to draw potential buyers in.'

'How is it weird? Lots of people live this way. I mean sure, it is…umm… yes, it's sterile, but that isn't so weird, is it?' The detective held back his frustration at the irrelevant avenue of conversation, he did not want his colleague's seemingly pointless comment to distract him… his mind was becoming lost, tired of waiting, unsure what to do next. He was secretly trying to keep his cool.

'Yeah. It's a couple who live here, no?'

The detective acknowledged Jonnah's question with a gentle nod which could have easily been mistaken for a slight nervous twitch.

'Well, there's also a girl who lives here too. A fourteen-year-old girl… but fuck me, would you believe it? There is seemingly no evidence she lives here… until you go digging through those mirrored wardrobes. This place is more than sterile, it's fucking weird, Detective.'

'I guess you're right.' Tim didn't like agreeing with Jonnah, it almost pained him, but he was a good detective and always listened to the thoughts of his team. 'Yeah, it is a little strange. Where are the family pictures? The dirty clothes strewn across the teenager's floor? The toys she used to play with that she cannot stand to let go? The make-up and accessories? Most teenage girls are a walking disaster area around the home.'

Jonnah had touched on something which became even more of an oddity the longer it brewed in Tim's mind.

The girl's behaviour was a little unusual also. On the outside she seemed to be upset, but not distraught, not the sort of uncontrollable, inconsolable, messed-up teenage girl that you would expect to find in a situation such as this. Tim had seen the damage these cases inflict on a person. Time after time he had seen the pain, the upset, the terror, the torment, but he failed to see any of that in this home... *shock perhaps?*

The detective walked towards the kitchen and stood covertly by the door, observing his officer's interactions with young Stephanie Barker. There were barely any words spoken between them, Sanders seemed to be looking around the kitchen awkwardly, unsure of what to say. Stephanie just sat quietly, a mug of hot chocolate in one hand, the other hand played with the curls in her long, dirty-brown hair. The look on her face was unreadable, free of any emotion. The girl's eyes were red and blotchy, showing signs of upset from a few tears shed upon their arrival. Her cheeks were a similar shade, but her mouth was still, no trembling, no uncomfortable movements trying to hold back the whines of a pained fourteen-year-old. The look in her eyes was cold, they slowly studied the room, examining the familiar surroundings with no signs of worry.

Tim's eyes met with Stephanie's, they locked with one another in a short stare before she casually smiled and took a sip of her drink.

'*Shock? Surely this is just shock, how is one meant to react to something as devastating as this?*' Tim pushed his thoughts to the back of his suspicious mind and returned to the living room to brief his team on the next course of action.

The team huddled around their superior as he detailed the protocols in an abduction scenario. He admitted that, during any case involving The Priest, there was very little to be done apart from wait for contact to be made. All they could do was watch; listen; record; report and hold on to every bit of hope they had. A separate team back at base were studying surveillance cameras around the city, searching for sightings or unusual behaviours. Details of the missing couple had been passed on to various media sources to spread the word to the public, but it was one of twelve missing persons cases reported in the city in the last two days, so coverage would be thinner than Tim would hope for.

Another concern was the lack of information about the couple to pass around, they seemed to live beneath the radar, blending into the crowd with little to no impact on their surroundings. No recent photos were found. One picture of them together at a new-years dinner party looked to be the most recent, but it was dated ten years prior.

The lack of data about the Barker's was the most unsettling for Tim, he knew the chances of a family reunion were draining by the minute... his resources were just as thin as the family's public image.

Regardless of his worries, Tim pushed on, attempting to breathe encouragement and hope into his team. He knew they all shared the same goal: return the parents to their daughter, unharmed. He promised his team he had every intention of driving the investigation with optimism and enthusiasm... they knew his words were empty, they knew the dark reality they faced.

During the briefing, Stephanie Barker sat alone at the kitchen table, silently, without any signs of distress... *'Shock! Surely the girl was just in shock?'*

3

Silence…

…it can make seconds feel like minutes…

…minutes feel like hours…

…hours feel like days...

…but days of continued radio silence, not even the annoying hiss of static... that feels like an eternity.

It was not unusual for Priest cases to be a monotonous trial of endurance. Experts had speculated that claiming responsibility for the abductions was just *'part of the game'*… a game which Tim Cropter did not enjoy playing. The thought of The Priest, or even a copycat, being involved in any abduction case he was working on, chilled him to the core… but it was the waiting which really tested his mettle.

The detective's nerves were just about holding together, but he was grateful for the hard-wearing flooring in the Barker residence. His pacing back and forth the sparse living room was a durability test of the carpet which manufacturers could not have foreseen.

The rest of the team kept themselves occupied in similar ways, be it twirling pens in their fingertips, staring out the window for hours on end, hiding behind their laptops in the pretence to be deep in research, or nose deep in a novel which had been stashed behind the guise of investigative case studies. The truth was, the team had been here before, stuck in the same situation, the same confused state, the same painful wait, watching the time pass them by, with no clue as to where to look first, it was simply a waiting game. Tim worried their time on the case would expire, resulting in an abandoned investigation. Stephanie Barker would then be bundled into the arms of the city's over-crowded, underfunded care system… as the days passed by, he saw it becoming a highly probable scenario.

The rest of the world flowed unknowingly around the apartment block, a stream of unrelenting chaos, a torrent of fluttering, lost souls. The bustling city never stood still, not for the Barker's, not for The Priest, and certainly not for Tim

Cropter. He knew his team wanted time to pass quickly, they had given up all hope, not that there were bucket loads of it to begin with. Often statistics spoke for themselves, they could not be ignored, there were countless families torn apart by the devastation of the city's psychopathic community... people went missing all too regularly, most never to be seen again.

Thirteen days of silence stuck inside a clinical, lifeless apartment was not Tim's idea of fun, it was totally alien to him how anyone could spend their lives in such a cold space. '*This is what happens to a child who grows up in a home like this, she is left just as cold and empty as the walls that enclose her.*' The thoughts kept floating through his head. He tried not to judge the young Barker girl, but her emotions were invisible... as if they had been throttled by an almost military style upbringing.

The standard protocol for an abduction was to return to the office at the end of the fourteenth day. This would allow Tim and his team just over twenty-seven hours, under normal circumstances. However, with every '*genuine*' Priest case, and copycats, the standard was usually silence until seventeen days after the victim's disappearance. Tim had already applied for the extended time and was certainly expecting to still be sleeping on the Barker's living-room floor until the final hour of that seventeenth day. If there was no news during the final day, the team would be required to leave the Barker's residence and hand Stephanie over to the officials, where she would spend the next four years in care. If the abductor were to make contact on the seventeenth day, the result would likely to be the same, as the Barker couple would undoubtedly already be deceased. Every member of Tim's 'missing persons unit' were expecting to pack up their belongings on day eighteen and to walk away with another 'unsolved'... it was a hard pill to swallow, but they all knew what to expect as soon as the call came in.

Officer Sanders had run through the routine questions with the Barker girl twice, asking the child what she had been doing whilst she waited for her parents to return from their shopping trip. Her answers were not unbelievable, but Tim decided he was going to ask the same questions and see if the replies matched.

'Steph?'

'Stephanie,' she corrected.

'Sorry, Stephanie... May I, err... may I sit at the table with you?'

'Certainly, Detective.'

'You seem very mature, Stephanie.'

'One must be, growing up in this city, in this area especially.'

'Well, I guess you are right there. You also seem to like sitting at this table. Would you not be more comfortable in the living room or your bedroom?'

'This is where the food is, plus it is where there happens to be less people congregating.'

Tim watched her face for signs of emotional damage, trauma, stress, worry... any emotion at all, but she continued to be a blank canvas.

'You seem to be a clever girl, Stephanie.'

'You seem to make a lot of assumptions, Detective.'

'Haha, yes, I guess I do, don't I? It is my job.'

He pulled out a small tube of mints from his shirt pocket, took one for himself before offering the packet across the table.

'Thank you.'

'Hey, take two, save me from myself,' he quickly snatched a second mint from the tube and dropped it into his mouth. 'Sweet tooth!' he exclaimed with a humoured smile.

'Gee, thanks.' Stephanie took two mints from the tube and promptly pushed them both through her pursed lips.

'*Progress!*' Tim thought to himself as the girl's face brightened, happily sucking the mints.

'Stephanie, can you tell me what you were doing whilst your parents were out please? Before you called us, that is.'

'You already know.' Stephanie's smile vanished and her face instantly drained of the newly expressed emotion.

'Humour me, please?'

'I was playing chess, on my own, against my virtual opponent. I had two games both lasting nearly three hours each. The computer records the length of games, how many moves each player makes, etcetera... that's when I realised the time and knew something was wrong.'

'Chess, hey? You good?'

'Level 173.'

'Wow, that sounds impressive' Tim chirped. 'You fancy a game?'

'You fancy losing, Detective?' Stephanie's head dipped, and an intent, devious sneer appeared on her face, she was clearly excited by the challenge.

'That's very unlikely, Stephanie. I will not be going easy on you.'

'I don't expect it.' Stephanie pulled out a small tablet shaped device from a drawer under the table and placed it between them. A quiet beep sounded. A projection of a holographic chess board in front of them. 'You are whites. It's your move, Detective Cropter.'

Tim realised he could question her over and over, but her answers would be carbon copies of the ones Sanders had already recorded.

She was a curiosity to the detective, he tried to find a sign of personality hidden behind her cold exterior, but she offered none... he hoped things would change after a few games. Knowing she was playing at level 173 on a near identical device he had at home, he was keen to challenge his level 171 skill against the cocky fourteen-year-old.

4

Chess: a game of strategy, of many complex variables and mathematics.

Chess: a game of patience, a game of planning ahead, achieving long-term positioning, and anticipating your opponent's every move.

Five games saw the evening lapse into the early hours of the morning. Five games of intense manoeuvres, cunning and skill. The first four games ended at two apiece. The fifth, a stalemate.

Tim Cropter and his team had been cooped up inside the Barker residence for two weeks and throughout Stephanie Barker, the daughter of Donald and Felicity, had shown very little sign of emotion. The young girl who had called the police when her parents never returned from a routine grocery run, never looked close to breaking. The little girl, who lived in a clean, sterile box, free of clutter, sparse of belongings, and generally deprived of any comforts to enrich one's personality, displayed no cracks in her calm, glacial persona... bar one initial outburst of tears at the very beginning, she was as cold as ice. That was until Detective Tim Cropter challenged her to a game of chess.

The first game was a quiet, peaceful affair, Tim took the win with relative ease and the game was finished in just under an hour. Stephanie came back fighting in the second, fuelled by her loss, the game lasted nearly two hours and saw Stephanie wrap Tim up in knots as she dominated and blocked his every move before finally cornering his white King. The third game gave Stephanie her second win of the evening... a long, closely fought game to the bitter end, one that neither player had felt sure of winning. The fourth game, was over in minutes and saw Stephanie concede another game to Tim, bringing them back onto level pegging. It was Tim's second win which gave him the results he desired: a break in Stephanie's immovable defences, a chink in her armour, a bullet through to a hidden blemish in her impenetrable stone soul.

As each game progressed, Stephanie became increasingly fidgety, but during the fourth game, Tim made it look as if she had never seen a chessboard before, and as Tim called 'checkmate', Stephanie Barker slammed her fist into the kitchen table with force and barked at the detective, demanding a rematch... a final decider.

'One more, we need one more game!' demanded the frustrated girl.

Tim was aware of the late hour, but he decided to be fair and accept the challenge of the fifth and final game.

'This is definitely the last game tonight, it's already late' he announced. He tried to make eye contact with his opponent, but she was clearly vexed and did everything in her power to avoid looking at him.

After he reset the playing pieces to their starting positions, ready for their showdown, the two contestants wasted no words and started their fifth and final game.

The game lasted far longer than Tim had anticipated, taking them up to the early hours of the morning. With the game reaching a climax, he noticed the room had started to fill with a musty glow of sunlight.

The detective closely observed the quiet, nonchalant child throughout the head- to-head, watching her reactions when placed under the pressure of losing to him for a possible third time. Despite her overwhelming competitive nature, she was unshakeable, bar a few words of frustration, she was totally focused on the game.

It was not the first time the thought had entered his head, but the detective had started to believe the girl's parents had fallen foul not to the mysterious criminal known as 'The Priest', but perhaps to Stephanie's own calculated and meticulously planned actions. The correct procedures had been followed to ensure the fourteen-year-old was included in the investigation from the start. The first rule of any criminal investigation is: everyone is a suspect, but the girl's story never broke, there were never any holes, no unanswered questions to cause any 'unusual concern', her story was flawless... *almost too perfect?* Tim had gone over many possibilities with his team, but there was no evidence to pin anything to the daughter of

Donald and Felicity Barker. The only lead was the phone call from The Priest claiming responsibility for the abduction. Voice analysis showed it was near identical to previous cases, but even the proven copycats could imitate the infamous digitally doctored vocal rhythms. The message sent to the police call centre was simply: 'You know who this is, don't you? I have Donald and Felicity Barker of The Garden District and you are all aware of what happens next!'

The 'standard' Priest message, as it had come to be known, had been widely published, meaning it was easy for any copycat to imitate... *but why would Stephanie? What would be her motive? Bad parenting perhaps? Was she feeling neglected throughout her dull existence by the two people who were supposed to show her love? Maybe it was for financial gain? Any assets would have been frozen until Stephanie turned eighteen and she would be placed under care for four years before she even got a sniff of any money. Perhaps she was just sick and twisted and yearned for the demise of her parents? Maybe she was not even responsible? Maybe it was a ridiculous notion, a misjudged step into a rabbit hole? Perhaps The Priest really was to blame, or some crazed fame seeking wannabe using his name? Maybe the fourteen days of silence and frustration had fucked up any rational thinking?*

It would not have been the first time the pressure of an abduction case had driven his imagination wild. In his job, it often paid to have a wandering imagination.

The cluster of suspecting thoughts tossed around inside Tim's head like a tornado tearing through a busy town, creating a scattering of confusion and panic in its wake. Right up to the move which saw Tim's last Pawn remove his opponent's final threat to his King, he carefully examined her behaviour.

The game ended as a draw and Stephanie's eyes glowed red as her face raged with fire, the teenager was furious at being unable to best the detective.

'Another game!' she demanded as Tim reset the chess pieces.

'No. It is already very late young lady, some games... you just cannot win!' The detective pressed the power button on the device and the chess board disappeared, reinforcing his decision to end their battle.

Tim turned his back on his impassioned opponent and stepped away from the dining table. A firm hand grasped his right wrist, interrupting him in his stride.

'You will never beat me detective… NEVER!' Her words were harrowing. Stephanie's face no longer raced with fire, she had become, once again, visibly void of any emotion. The young girl's grip was notably strong and assertive, she wanted to be clear about who was in control of their current situation, showing her true colours to the detective and giving him the answer to his troubling suspicions.

'You haven't won here, Stephanie, not in this game, nor in the other game. You may think you can beat the system. You may think you can beat me, but I don't give up easily.'

'I will find a way to beat you, Detective Cropter!'

'No, Stephanie. It is I who will find a way to win this game. This is what I do. I know who you are now Miss Barker, I know what you are capable of.' The detective yanked at his arm, pulling away from the girl's grasp. 'I will be watching you, Miss Barker! I will be watching… and I will beat you, mark my words!' The detective tapped the light switch as he left the kitchen, leaving Stephanie in darkness.

Stephanie Barker, daughter of 'missing' Donald and Felicity, fourteen years of age, a chess skill of 173, and a girl capable of intense planning and cunning, sat in silence in the pitch-black kitchen, contemplating her next move.

5

The team packed away their clutter of surveillance equipment littering the apartment. Tim was aware Stephanie stood behind him, drawing imaginary daggers in his back. Despite the lack of hours on the living room floor, he had slept well. His mood that morning was as calm as it was throughout the evening of chess. He was cautious of his revelations and aware of his lack of evidence. The chances that anyone would have faith in his suspicions about a child being responsible for her parents' disappearance due to her behaviour during a few games of chess, was not just slim, it was anorexic. Experience told him he had to be wary about throwing around accusations without real proof. It was not implausible for a person of Stephanie's age to commit a serious crime against their family, even their parents, but it was common for a media frenzy to spiral uncontrollably when The Priest, or one of his copy-cats had been thrown into the pool of suspects in an abduction case. Tim knew there were always leaks in the department, always individuals who were willing to sell information to the press, without enough evidence to pin the Barker's disappearance on their glacial daughter, his best option was to keep tight-lipped until he could pile some weight behind his theory. He knew that despite his gut instinct, it was all just theory.

'A team will be along soon to take you into care Stephanie. I am sorry we have not been able to help much you so far, but we will not give up.' Officer Jonnah placed his hand upon Stephanie's shoulder to add some physical comfort to his words.

'It's not your fault, I know you are doing your best.'

Stephanie's reply to the officer did not go unnoticed by Tim, neither did her tone. The detective did not have to look at her to know her face was deadpan… he could hear it. He noted the lack of concern, the lack of worry, the absence of any distress for her parents' wellbeing and even of her own. She was about to be shipped off into care, removed from her home, separated from her past, discarded like an unwanted gift, and yet she was still stone cold.

'Hey, Stephanie! Could you come here a minute, please?' Tim called out, walking into the kitchen.

'Detective?' she asked, walking behind him.

Tim picked up the chess device from the dining table and handed it to her.

'Don't forget this...' he paused looking deep into her eyes. 'For the next time you want to play games.'

'Perhaps you should keep it, Tim... for the next time you wish to try and outwit me.' Stephanie folded her arms behind her back, refusing to take the device.

The pair stood for a few seconds in restraint, locked in a defiant stare which neither one wanted to withdraw from.

'Stephanie, do you think you have won?' Tim asked, offering the chess set once more.

'Is it a case of winning and losing, Tim? Do you really wish to better a child? Because it seems to me you are incapable of doing so!' A rare smirk appeared on her face as she gloated to her opponent.

'I ask you again, Stephanie...' Tim cast the chess set onto the dining table and tucked his hands into his trouser pockets. 'Do you think that you have won? You're about to be taken into care, your life has been turned upside down and the future ahead of you hangs in the balance, full of uncertainty. Do you truly believe you have won here?'

Stephanie did not react to the detective's words, her stare remained intense, her gaze locked with his.

'I thought so. You understand exactly what is happening here, don't you? I feel...'

A barrage of gunfire interrupted Tim's speech followed by the ear shattering, harrowing screams of his team in the next room.

Tim launched himself towards Stephanie and pulled her to the floor in one swift motion, using his body as shield without hesitation.

'Stay calm, Stephanie!' Tim pleaded as he pulled his large automatic pistol from his jacket.

Fragments of internal walls spat across the kitchen, showering them both in dust. The sound of bullets cutting through the air zipped around them.

'WHAT THE FUCK IS GOING ON?' Tim shouted to his team. 'HEY, REPORT?' He waited briefly for an answer but all that returned in reply was the sound of a stun grenade. His brain rattled in his skull as the blast assaulted his senses.

The daze was hard to shake off.

He worked to gather himself and fight against the pressure in his skull. He could feel blood begin to trickle from his left ear… permanent hearing damage was almost certain.

The body of Officer Sanders flew through the kitchen doorway, sliding across the floor. Tim rushed to her side, but the clear tunnel through her skull offered explanation to her swift entry into the kitchen as well as confirming her demise.

Tim threw himself into the living room and returned fire to the direction of his attackers outside. He did not have time to question if it was skill or luck which took down one of the gunmen with his first shot, but he wasted no time in throwing his back to the wall to find cover. A quick scan of the living room told him his odds of survival: every team member was down, only Jonnah was left alive, but he was full of holes, leaking blood and in plain sight of the window… *too much of a risk to try and attend to him*.

The hearing damage and the continued gunfire drowned Jonnah's screams, but the pain was clearly visible on his face.

'Fuck!' Tim muttered as he watched his team member writhe in pain. 'I'm sorry, Jonnah!' he cried, sobbing as he watched two more bullets pump into the officer's body.

Tim reached out and removed a revolver from the holster of another fallen team member.

He checked the gun, it was equipped with a small telescopic sight and fully loaded, its owner never even managed to get off a shot.

He waited for the gunfire to ease before making a dash to the nearby bedroom. A bullet clipped his right calf before he could get clear of the doorway.

He winced in pain. The wound was clean and hurt like hell, a far too familiar pain for Tim. He had taken a bullet before, luckily this shot was only a graze in comparison.

The barrage continued. The Barker's residence was under

a heavy assault that shook the entire buildings foundations.

Tim scanned the bedroom frantically. The mirrored walls were perfect to provide a clear picture of the apartment. The array of reflections also offered him a perfect view through the kitchen doorway. Stephanie had taken cover behind one of the kitchen units and seemed to be clear of any immediate danger.

With Tim's team all out of the picture, the onslaught of gunfire concentrated in his immediate direction, the obvious tactic was to take out the police presence first, before making a move on the girl.

The walls of mirrored glass also gave him the ability to capture a glimpse of his enemies: three gunmen were in sight, armed with automatic rifles and suited up in full tactical body armour. He was unable to see the body of the gunman he had hit, but he was certain it was a kill shot... not many people could survive a burst of gunfire above the shoulder line.

The thunderous roar of gunfire ceased, replaced by the immutable ringing of permanent eardrum damage. The air around him had been consumed by thick clouds of dust and gunpowder smoke.

Tim swallowed hard, holding back the phlegm and filth trying to escape his lungs.

Through the incessant ringing he could make out the sound of rubble cracking beneath the feet of the approaching attackers as they cautiously made their way into the apartment. Tim knew he had to act fast, time was running out, he knew they would commence fire at the slightest sign of life. Undoubtedly the small squad of assassins would be looking to flee the scene promptly: despite the overwhelming workload caving in over the city's police department, the disappearance of the Barker's placed The Garden District under high alert, which meant backup was likely to be already on the way.

Tim knew he had to act fast.

He frantically scanned the mirrors again for a glimpse of any targets.

Through the haze of thick dust clouds, the outline of two gunmen appeared, walking side-by-side... this was Tim's one and only chance.

He threw his back into the mirrored wall behind him and squeezed the trigger of his gun, firing off eight armoured piercing rounds through the interior wall.

The bullets smashed into the living room and found their targets with ease, '*all those nights at the range did you good, Cropter',* he thought to himself, listening to the screams of his adversaries.

'WHAT THE FUCK? YOU BASTARD! I'M GOING TO...' the furious howl of a fourth assassin gave Tim a good estimation where to fire his next shots. He emptied the last of his clip in a concentrated spread of fire, aiming at the general direction of the voice which had just called out to him.

Tim reloaded his gun without hesitation. He calmed his mind, slowed his breathing and kept still, patiently waiting for the next sound. A quiet thud informed him he had found his target... '*a stroke of luck or great instincts?'...* he was not going to waste time trying to decide which.

The detective sprung to his feet and shuffled awkwardly across the bedroom floor, heading towards the doorway to check for further threats. His leg throbbed but he did not have the time to cry about it.

The living room was in chaos, bodies littered the floor, showered in debris and splashed with enough red to create a large painting.

Every member of Tim's team was motionless, the hit on them was almost a total success, but they never planned for Tim's reaction and perfect accuracy, the sharpshooting detective executed all four heavily armed combatants with relative ease.

'Stephanie? Hey, are you hurt?' asked Tim as he checked the windows.

The coast seemed to be clear, the streets were cluttered with curious, panicked neighbours, desperate to catch a glimpse of the action.

'I am unharmed' she replied.

Tim noted once again the lack of concern in her voice, the lack of fear, '*perhaps she was just raised without emotion, without a care for anything? Perhaps the detective was wrong? Who had the death-squad come to kill?'*

Tim's thoughts were interrupted by a heavy blow to his back, thrusting him forward. A bullet burst through his torso and drove into the wall in front of him before he collapsed to the floor.

His own blood had splashed his face…

…he could taste it…

… that metallic taste that was simply unmistakeable.

Sharp spasms shot through his body as he screamed out in agonising, wrenching pain.

He reached out for his dropped weapon… fingernails clawing frantically at the floor.

His head spun like it was too heavy for his shoulders. His eyes rolled around like marbles in a jar. Vomit boiled in his throat.

He clenched his lips, desperate to hold the contents of his stomach down.

His left hand found his gun, he grabbed at it and attempted to roll over, but his body was becoming numb, he was losing all control below his hips.

'AAAH, FUCK! FUCK, FUCK…. FUCK!' he screamed as his eyes attempted to hunt for the shooter amongst the carnage in the once immaculate apartment.

'You… you will regret this!' a weak voice announced. 'You have no idea who we are!'

Tim's ears pinpointed the direction of the pitiful voice and he immediately fired hysterically towards it.

The three bullets found their target: an injured gunman who survived the marksman's shots from the bedroom… Tim's frantic, blind shots had finally laid him to rest.

'Detective Cropter?' Stephanie called out as she walked towards the failing policeman.

Sirens wailed through the apartment as Tim's backup arrived, moments too late.

The detective's eyes flickered as he began to lose consciousness.

Amongst the sirens and the chaos of the approaching medical team, Tim could hear the detached tone of Stephanie's voice…

'Detective, you're still alive?'

6

As a member of the city's police department, injury in line of duty grants no medal. There is no award ceremony to congratulate your honour and valour. There is no collective gathering of the 'city's finest', ready to pat you on the back and raise a glass in your name... there is only despair.

The despair that hits when you realise you were just a number in an overworked arm of law-enforcement.

A despair brought on by the overwhelming devastation that you will never be able to work again... never serve the city again.

The despair that your life has changed, and things will never be the same again.

The despair hit Tim worse than anyone would have ever imagined: solitude, depression, nightmares, several failed suicide attempts, Tim Cropter suffered it all.

The bullet which drilled through his spine, took away the use of his legs. It paralysed him from the hip down.

Anger consumed him.

Rage tortured him.

Fear became him.

Tim spent years trying to learn the fate of the Barker's, trying to find the people responsible for the deaths of his team members. He pleaded with the care authorities to allow him to further question Stephanie Barker, convinced she must know more than she had let on.

All the official lines of questioning were extinguished after the firefight had taken him and his team out of service.

Three years after the Barker's disappearance, all the unofficial backdoors into the investigation, which could be opened by greasing a few palms, were also closed to the former detective.

Years of psychiatric care helped numb the suffering to a degree, but it was never enough to help Tim sleep at night. The case may have been closed shortly after the firefight, but he kept pushing, pressing his contacts, both in the department and on the streets, for information, but the leads went nowhere… It drove him mad.

Then Stephanie died.

When he was informed of her passing, Tim pressed even harder on his contacts for any information into her death… but was thwarted at every turn.

No one wanted to discuss it.

The Barker daughter had been unreachable since the massacre at the apartment, her identity had been changed and she was hidden from everyone, including those previously involved with the case.

A media uproar had exploded after the firefight and the city's Mayor decided to do what he did best… brush it all under the carpet.

The Priest abductions continued for a further two years, and then… suddenly ceased.

No one was ever convicted for 'The Priest' crimes, only the copycats. Theories circulated The Priest never even existed, people speculated it was just a group of individuals copying an idea, turning it into an institution. Whatever happened, it nearly cost Tim Cropter his sanity.

The government housed him in an apartment block on the ground floor, allowing him easy access with his wheelchair, but the masses of civilians outside his windows only drove him more insane. The hustle and bustle of the millions in the city was enough to drive most people mad, let alone a fixated, crippled, recluse in search of the invisible.

Tim closed himself off from the world, keeping himself in the darkness of his apartment, curtains drawn and rarely venturing outside. It was not until he found love that he could remove his focus from 'the Barker events'.

Ezme Robart was in many ways his saviour, she freed him from the darkness, from his turmoil, from his obsession.

The couple met at a bar which had become one of Tim's few weekly haunts.

'Syd's Watering Hole' was lost somewhere between being an upmarket bar and a decaying old boozer. The owner, Syd, had passed away after suffering from a heart-attack during a poorly executed armed-robbery attempt by three masked men. The armed men tried to gain entry through the locked side door of the crowded bar, drawing immediate attention to themselves. Syd, bemused, went out to investigate the commotion, and was subsequently beaten down in the middle of the street. The would-be robbers barged into the bar, and demanded Syd's takings, but left with only a small handful of 'credit-tokens', due to Syd having completed his weekly bank-run only two hours prior.

The day of the botched robbery was the first time Tim had been in the bar, he had witnessed the whole event unfold, but he failed to act. After drinking half a bottle of vodka at home that evening, he swore to himself he would visit the bar the same day each week, in the hope that Syd's killers would return. He swore that despite being confined to his wheelchair, he would find the culprits and serve justice to the three masked men... after the second half of the vodka bottle... Tim only ever remembered the first part of his promise to himself.

Tim Cropter had met many people in the bar, mainly contacts which he hoped would provide him with leads in the Barker case, but no one had ever made an impression on him like *Ezme Robart*.

He would often reminisce about the first time he saw her. She stood out not for her physical looks, but for the long, purple coat she wore that day... as she entered the bar, her coat followed her in slow-motion, swaying with each step, an image which stayed with Tim always.

The day they bumped into each other, was the day Tim decided to begin living again.

7

'Well, don't you look dapper today!' Tim called out as Ezme walked towards him, having just entered 'Syd's Watering Hole' to join him for their weekly lunchtime drink.

'Thank you, babe. You don't look too bad yourself!'

Ezme shone in a purple, velvet suit. Her short hair had been manipulated with wax to create a uniform pattern of spikes. Her hair was coloured just a shade darker than the purple of her suit. A pair of thick-rimmed glasses complimented her bright green eyes. She openly admitted she only wore glasses for cosmetic reasons, her eyesight was near perfect, but she felt the spectacles gave her a hint of femininity she had lost with her 'boyish' hairstyle and lack of 'girly' clothing. A black shirt under her jacket hugged her hidden curves and a pair of heavy, black work-boots beneath her trousers finished off the look that had Tim smiling like a crazed love-struck loon.

Ezme often brought a smile to his face. Before they had met, he hadn't smiled for a long time, but when the two were together, all of Tim's nightmares seemed to be long forgotten memories.

'How many have you had, Tim?'

'Why, because I am paying you a compliment?' He laughed, tickled by her jibe. He signalled to the barkeep and asked for Ezme's usual tipple: a strawberry liqueur shaken with a dash of pineapple soda.

'Thanks, I appreciate your comments, as always. How has your day been?' She raised a small, yet gleeful smile and winked at Tim, thanking him for the drink and giving him her approval as she took a moment to savour the fruity flavours.

'It has been a quiet day,' Tim studied the brushed steel bar top, losing himself in a moment as he tried to remember the colourless events of his morning 'just a normal day.'

'Wow, just a normal day? You say this with a hint of dejection.'

'It is just a normal bloody day, nothing unusual has happened, not to me anyway.' A quick blast of vodka did not help him to acknowledge any significant events of the day. 'I do get to see you, which is obviously something that brightens up my day.'

'Today is a special day, Tim... You don't remember why?'

A period of embarrassing confusion passed over him as he searched Ezme's blank face for a clue. A nervous laugh broke out, his face contorted like a rung-out dishcloth as he battled with the question which he was clearly meant to have the answer to.

'Another round please, Tim's paying!' A fresh smile appeared on her face as she watched her partner squirm uncomfortably on his barstool. She thanked the barkeep and handed over her payment card. 'There's not much left on there, put the rest in the tips, please?'

'Thank you, ma'am,' replied the barkeep before dashing over to the payment terminal to check the value of the tip.

Tipping was rare, but both Tim and Ezme always tried to oblige when they could.

'I HAVE GOT IT!' Tim announced with a burst of joy 'It's been three years! Three years since I met you, and it was right here, in this exact spot... well almost.'

'Ha! That's right is it?'

'Well, yeah? It is isn't it?' Tim finished the first glass of vodka and poured the second into his original glass, a habit he always questioned but never changed. His vodka was always a double, he could drink like a fish, partly because the cocktail of medicines counteracted the effects of the alcohol, and partly because, even around Ezme, he still liked to numb the pains of his injury, both physically and mentally. The vodka was always straight, and he sipped it to savour the taste, a taste this partner always questioned with confusion.

'If you say so.' Ezme placed a hand on Tim's shoulder and rubbed him playfully.

'Well, I know it was three years today, but is this what you were referring to?'

'If this is what you say today is, then this is what today must be.'

'You fucking wind-up, you.'

'Ha! A wind-up, me?' Ezme cackled before finishing her

drink. She slid off her stool and walked over to the jukebox in the corner. Both were fans of traditional R&B and Soul music, Tim was proud of his knowledge of music and had been an avid collector throughout his life, his music library was expansive and often the talking point for the couple.

She tapped a series of commands on the jukebox screen, picking a selection of her favourite songs. The jukebox was a simple floating, holographic panel, projected from a small box on the wall, it was an archaic design, in-keeping with the rest of the décor in 'Syd's'. A total of sixteen speakers scattered the ceiling of the bar, capable of filling the establishment with an adequate sound.

The first song began with a slow saxophone introduction and Ezme began to move with the music, rolling her body gently, from her shoulders down to her hips.

A quiet drumbeat kicked in, as did the rest of Ezme's body, moving like an enchanted snake, rolling and gyrating... the actions of a sensual belly dancer.

For the first thirty-five seconds she kept her back to him, her hands ran sensually up and down her thighs in time with her dance.

Tim had never seen his partner so much as nod her head to music, let alone twist and turn like a smooth temptress in a bar half-full of people.

He watched in awe as her body rotated in his direction, still gyrating and rolling. The rest of the bar began to pay attention to her dance, she stood out a mile amongst the generally morose patrons of 'Syd's Watering Hole'. Her face radiated with pure joy, she rarely showed emotion, but it was clear whatever she was thinking as she danced to the sounds of the jukebox, she had become lost in the moment.

Tim questioned his eyes, it seemed to be completely out of character for the woman he had been dating for three years to suddenly begin a provocative dance in the middle of a bar.

In his company, she had always been a fun person, always laughing and joking in private, but very reserved in public. Even in private, he had never seen her dance, other than a few awkward steps whilst acting a fool in the confines of his home.

The loss of sensation in his lower body, meant he could never be aroused by his partner in the way he wished he could, he yearned for the intimacy he believed couples should share: *the closeness, the togetherness*. His disability did not stop the mental stimulation he received whenever he was in Ezme's company, her presence was invigorating.

Ezme's dance continued into the second song, picking up pace into more vigorous movements. The higher tempo and faster, more powerful movements aroused Tim even more than the first dance. He watched in silence, a beaming smile on his face, flush with the feeling of complete adoration, yet he felt a hint of embarrassment by his almost predatory lust.

As the second song reached the final climax, his desires crumbled beneath the realisation that not only could he never share real intimacy with his love, but it also dawned on him that the ability to get up and dance in front of a room full of strangers was another luxury stolen from him by a bullet..

'Hey… Don't be sad!' Ezme called over to Tim as she shuffled towards him, her hips still moving to the final few beats of the song.

'Me? Never!' he shrugged before finishing another vodka.

'I know that look. That sombre look you often wear on your face. Have another drink, then we'll hit the road.'

'Where are we going?'

'Back to your place, Mr Cropter…' Ezme signalled for another drink and returned to the stool next to her partner. 'One more drink, then back to your place' her eyes flicked to her left, drawing Tim's attention to a pink shopping bag he failed to notice upon her arrival. 'I have a surprise for you!'

'Oh, really?' he blushed.

Tim tried to sneak a look into the bag, but Ezme's foot dragged it away from his view.

'No peaking, Mr Cropter!'

He continued to blush, embarrassed and excited by the thoughts of what was waiting for him in the bag. Suddenly aware of his fixation on the bag, he pulled his mind out of the gutter and awkwardly scanned the bar, desperate to find a new distraction.

Ezme giggled at the sight of Tim's obvious discomfort.

It did not take long until Tim found his distraction: over Ezme's right shoulder a man in his late fifties watched on, deep in concentration behind a pair of blue-tinted glasses. It dawned on Tim the man had been watching them closely since Ezme's arrival, yet Tim failed to recognise how intent the man's voyeurism had become.

'Errr… time for another? Just one more?' Tim asked nervously, trying to buy more time to assess the situation and question his imagination.

'Another? You have a fresh one in your hand.'

Tim began to feel anxious and uncomfortable. He could feel his palms becoming sweaty and a prickly heat blooming on his cheeks. He became angry with himself, asking how he had failed to spot the voyeur sooner? An imaginary database of mugshots flickered away inside his head, frantically scanning for a match to the man in the corner of Syd's.

'How could you let your guard down in such a way? You don't serve as a cop for years without making enemies. Just because you leave as a cripple, it doesn't mean your enemies will show any remorse, any compassion. It doesn't mean they will suddenly forget you… every officer in the department made enemies, they just prayed never to meet them again… Fuck, now Ezme could be in real danger!' Tim's mind fluttered like a panicked moth in a shot glass. He could feel the voyeur watching their every move.

'Tim? You look distracted!' Ezme asked, seemingly unaware of the panic stations alarming in his head.

'Ummm… yeah! I just think maybe we should have one more.' Tim reached behind him, checking his chair for his stashed gun. Ezme had always protested her disgust for firearms, but old habits die hard. Almost every ex-police personnel kept themselves armed… just in-case.

His fingertips found the grip of his revolver, the texture of the engraved grip eased him slightly and he returned to his drink, one eye focused on the voyeur in the corner and his mind focused on the revolver.

The following twenty minutes dragged by, Tim had become completely distracted by the voyeur and failed to engage in any conversations with Ezme, other than a few grunts and groans.

The voyeur continued to slowly sip away at his drink, making the pint last longer than most people would empty an entire barrel of beer. He pretended to read an old book from the bookshelf by the window, but along with the tinted glasses, the literature only acted as another cover for his shady green eyes.

'Tim, it's time to go home!' Ezme announced as she bounced from her stool. 'Come, let's go to yours and enjoy the rest of this special day.'

'Yes… yes of course' he replied anxiously.

The voyeur lowered his book and became visibly more interested in their movements.

Ezme thanked the landlord and made her way to the door. Tim followed closely, keeping the voyeur in his field of vision.

The city air hit Tim like a wrecking ball as the door to Syd's slammed behind him.

A shudder rushed through him, the alcohol reminding him he had surpassed his limitations.

'Fuck! That's bright.' Tim declared, shielding his eyes from the glaring sun.

'How many did you have, Tim?'

Tim spun his wheelchair 180 degrees, expecting the voyeur to appear. *'Shit, you are imagining things!'*

'Tim?'

'Too many' he snapped. 'Clearly I have had one too many.' Tim turned his chair and hurried along to catch up with Ezme.

'Clearly!' she chuckled, leading the way home.

8

Tim sat at his dining table shaking his head, trying to shrug off the many vodkas from Syd's.

The sense of being watched stayed with him all the way to his apartment door, but there was no sign of anyone following them, despite his suspicions. His lack of full-body mobility made it very difficult to keep an eye on his surroundings, but he was sure they had made their way home alone.

His cautions made the first twenty minutes after their arrival home rather awkward, he sat quietly at the dining table keeping his eyes peeled for any signs of danger. He had contemplated calling Ezme a taxi to take her home but figured she was probably safer with him... his mobility skills may have been lacking, but his marksmanship was still on top form, thanks to his weekly visits to the gun range.

'Tim, will you stop looking over at the door, please?'

'Oh shit, sorry. I guess I am just feeling that damn vodka.'

'Yes, you have been shaking your head repeatedly since we left Syd's.' Ezme laughed and reached across the table to hold his hand, to which he accepted.

Her hand was warm to touch, Tim's condition meant poor circulation, making his hands feel like ice blocks in any temperature, but he could feel the warmth in her skin.

'I'll just get you a glass of juice on my way to the bedroom.'

'Are you going to bed already, Ezme?'

'No, I just want to sort out your surprise' she replied as she walked into the open-plan kitchen area.

Tim rubbed his hands together trying to generate heat and get the blood moving, he figured they might be needed when his received his surprise.

'Here, take these and drink up!'

He thanked her for the drink and the two tablets she placed on the table in front of him, before placing them onto his tongue and swallowing them dry. The first slipped down easy but the second lodged in his throat, it took almost a full pint of juice to wash it down. 'Dick!' he said out-loud, amazed at his own stupidity.

Ten minutes passed and Ezme was still in the bedroom clambering around, making enough noise for Tim's excitement levels to start rising.

A black clock hung on the wall in front of him, it was given to him by his father, not because it was an heirloom, but simply because as a child Tim had been terrible at being prompt with his arrangements.

He stared at the clock and became lost in memories of his father shouting at him for being late home, he was a hard man, but a fair one.

He shook his head, attempting to snap back to reality.

His eyelids began to feel weak and his head became a heavy weight on his shoulders. The clock hands seemed to slow to almost a halt as drowsiness kicked in, *'Shit! One vodka too many!'*

9

Tim woke to the sound of a chair being dragged across the dining room floor.

He rocked his head side to side trying to bring himself round, but a heavy haze weighed on his brain.

He looked up to see Ezme sit herself down at the other end of the table, with the pink shopping bag in front of her.

'Finally, you're awake!'

He opened his mouth and searched for a reply but failed to make a sound.

'Ah shit, you've lost your voice? That's to be expected. I guess you feel like shit, huh? Pretty hazy?'

Tim attempted to lift his hands to his face, but his brain was failing to command his arms to function.

'So, here we are. I want to talk to you, tell you a story.' Ezme pushed the bag to the side of the table and leaned back in her chair 'You see, for three years I have been here through your suffering. I have waited for you to get better. I have waited for you to sleep… I mean really sleep. Your nightmares keep you awake at night. You have improved… over the years you certainly have improved, but you still suffer. Do you want me to tell you this story, one which may help you sleep?' She sat calm, gently caressing the table in front of her with her fingertips.

Tim tried to speak, but his speech was yet to wake.

He turned his attention to the clock, he had slept for five hours, probably the deepest sleep he had experienced in years, but his brain felt like it had been removed and replaced by a ball of mushy goo.

His thoughts turned the voyeur in the bar, he questioned whether he had imagined the whole event, whether he was cracking up… thinking about it only made him more confused.

He turned his attention back to Ezme, the smile she wore so proudly in the bar had vanished, replaced by a blank expression. His docile brain guessed she was pretty pissed at him drinking too heavily and for ruining their special day by freaking out over a random patron in a bar.

Ezme cleared her throat, focused on Tim and began her story.

'Years ago, there was this idea, more of a realisation, really. The city we live in is rife with decay, consumed by greed, swamped in filth. I don't wish to bore you too much with the history of it all, but basically... a plan was born to eradicate this filth. A collective took it upon themselves to find the people who were hiding in plain sight, the ones who simply did not deserve the lives they had been blessed with. You know, there is a God, he did not wish for his children to become animals, but they did anyway, despite his best efforts. So, this group, they took the scum, the guilty, and they hunted them... they hunted them like the animals they were. On the streets, in the sewers, they even took them out to the country, and they hunted them. The idea was great, thousands of worthless sub-humans have been wiped clean from existence, and there are always plenty of good folk just waiting to help with the cleansing. They too wanted to buy into the idea for a greater way of life. Every time the group have been discovered, every time they met resistance, they changed strategies. It has become a tradition, the hunts. I'm sure you have heard of them, as an ex-law enforcer, you must have at least heard rumours, the legends?'

Tim's head continued to roll on his shoulders as he struggled to regain full consciousness, he listened to Ezme's words, but his head was filled with confusion. He tried once again to speak but only managed a low grumble in his throat.

'There are bad people about, Tim. There are a lot of bad, bad people and the police, they do very little to keep us safe... they fail to right the wrongs.'

'Ez... wha....?' Grunted Tim, as he began to regain control of his vocal cords.

'What am I talking about? Is that what you are trying to say?' she waited for his response... a wobbly nod of his head was all he could manage.

'The Priest, you remember? Don't you, Tim? You see, there never was a Priest, well... not really. The Priest was a horror story, you know, like the boogie man. A story you tell people to keep them from the truth. My father told me about the boogie man. He told me the boogie man was the reason for my nightmares… ironic really, isn't it babe?'

Ezme opened the pink shopping bag and reached inside.

'I told you today was a special day, didn't I? To be honest I am shocked you don't remember such a significant event.'

Consciousness battled with the confusion inside Tim's head, he asked himself if he was dreaming, but could not move to pinch himself to test.

'Ten years ago… that's when you met your boogie man for the first time, wasn't it? That's when your nightmares began, when The Priest came knocking on your door? That's when it all began?'

Ezme removed a small, silver box from the bag and gently placed it in the centre of the table, it was shiny and new, no markings or logos, with just a small red button positioned on the top.

'My father, he told me not to be afraid of the boogie man. He told me that if I never talked about it, he would cease to exist. My mother, she knew about the boogie man, she knew the things he did to me, and she ignored his existence, but he never went away, he still existed… until I found a group of people who offered to help me. I bet your therapist told you to forget about your boogie man, hey, Tim? Did she tell you to deny his existence?'

Tim's heart sank as the jigsaw pieces began to drop into place.

His brain was wide awake and functioning to full capacity, his voice was back, but he could not speak.

The last three years of his life, fond new memories had helped him forget the events which married him to his chair. Memories which clouded the events that stole the use of his legs… they evaporated into the dark, clouded atmosphere, absorbed by a harsh new reality.

'I know you don't recognise the face you see before you. I know you have a lot of questions you want to ask… but we both know… I won't answer them. I shouldn't really need to. You denied me entry to the group, Tim. I was meant to leave that day. I was meant to go and join them, to face the boogie man… but you had to play games.'

Tim felt his arms tingle, the sensations were coming back, his upper body was beginning to awake.

He examined her face, staring deep into her eyes, but she was cold, expressionless… void from any emotions.

'It took me a while, a long time in fact… but I found a way to beat you, Detective Cropter,' Ezme boasted as she pressed the small red button on the box.

A faint beep sounded from the box and a small white light flickered, illuminating a large hologram above it, spanning most of the dining table.

'You are whites… It's your move, Detective!'

Chess: a game of strategy, of many complex variables and mathematics.

Chess: a game of patience, a game of planning ahead, achieving long-term positioning, and anticipating your opponent's every move.

ANOTHER GAME OF CHESS
BY **TERRY KING & CHERALYN MAY**

Judgement of the Faceless

Part Two

We reconnect with our heroes as they roar through the night on another high-octane mission to avenge the ones harmed by the cruel acts of the digitally enabled cowards. The cowards who hide behind screens, spreading their words of venom and hatred. These cowards believe they are safe, masking their digital identities and blurring their trails with hi-tech trickery... Our heroes ride through the night to remind the cowards: their crimes are not without reprisal.

Our merciless duo recently laid to waste a triplet of odious teenagers that used their repugnant minds to prey on their fellow students. They taunted the weak minded by attacking them with constant, harrowing and abusive threats, sending words of hatred to their personal communicators. Brick suppressed two of the disgusting teens with a helping hand from *Penny*: her two-handed mallet. Ram neutralised the third teen by means of swift decapitation.

On to their second mission of the night... Ram and Brick leave the dizzying heights of the overpass behind them and take to the city's sewer system. The city's high-rise motorway had been crawling with an army of police after a violent block war spilled onto the roads on the west side of the city. The chaos of the block war would have given the police a taste for blood, a hunger to bring down anyone who challenged the law and our heroes knew it and knew that it was best to avoid the futile grounds of the overpass.

The two nitrous injected machines rumbled along the dark passages beneath the city streets. The high-intensity main-beam from Ram's bike illuminated the pitch-black path ahead. Faint trails of neon light lay stagnant behind them. Sprays of storm water flick from the rear tyres and into the spoiled air, scattering the light trails, creating an abstract canvas reminiscent of a timeless, noir movie poster. Half of the city's waste runs through a maze of pipework that weaves beneath the tunnel floors - the other half lays stagnant in the city above... waiting for their day of reckoning.

225

The tunnels give our heroes a swift route through the city, but the sharp turns and narrow passages add a new sense of danger to their mission that both riders cannot help but rejoice in - wailing and hollering like excited children.

Our heroes have tracked the activities of this sinister online group for longer than they care to admit. Their usual tracking techniques had been unsuccessful against the groups' complex systems, pushing our duos determination beyond any levels we have previously witnessed. Nevertheless, through determination and grit, Ram and Brick had successfully pinned this particularly heinous collective to the Gualtony Towers.

An unknown number of perpetrators reside on the 6th floor of Gualtony Tower Block-B. Ram's entry to the 6th floor is by taking the stairs. The building trembles as he manoeuvres his ravenous bike along a series of staircases and corridors at violent and terrifying speeds. The bikes' decorative lighting illuminates the walls with a glorious yellow-neon glow. Ram crucifies the silent building with blips of emotional throttle, before performing an aerial dismount that propels him through the door of apartment 6234. The hero rolls through the entrance to the apartment and stands strong, spinning his swords in a display of true weapon mastery.

Brick's approach is once again less flamboyant than her partner's. The biker finds her way onto a neighbouring rooftop that creates the perfect launch pad to gain entry through the apartment's large living-room windows. Brick powers through the city sky, pulling back on the handles of the airborne bike. Her bike splinters both windows from their hinges and sends the framed plexi-glass across the living-room of the apartment in a glorious cyclone fashion, the stunt had been perfectly executed by the skilled biker. One of the airborne window frames travels across the room and pummels into a lone female perpetrator, crushing her head against a large computer screen: perhaps the most fitting death for a cyber bully?

Brick casually dismounts, unperturbed by her recent kill. She clutches *Penny* in both hands, ready to create more devastation. Ram nods in appreciation of her riding skill and deadly efficiency, then joins her side, also poised for the next kill.

A herd of wild animals could not disguise the noise in the neighbouring room: the familiar sound of the guilty, scurrying, panicking, fearing their impending doom.

Ram and Brick master the art of surprise on their missions and have never encountered any resistance from the guilty, beyond a few minor scuffles... but today is a different day. A scattering of pellets blasts a large hole in the wall in front of them. Brick reacts and dives to the carpeted floor as a second blast narrowly misses her helmet. Ram's reaction is just as instantaneous: he hurls three throwing knives through the void in the wall, the first one misses and imbeds into a poster of a retro pop-band, the other two punch into the chest of another female perp, creating a tortured scream from the blonde-haired woman that bellows through the apartment.

Brick springs to her feet and sets to the wall, *Penny* flailing in front of her like an efficiently destructive mining machine. The heavy mallet disintegrates the interior divide, revealing four petrified, unarmed women and a fifth - desperately trying to reload her spent shotgun. Brick examines the room of screens, each one littered with pictures. Each picture is a pornographic display of women, stolen from personal computers, and communicators, ready to be distributed online or sold to the highest bidder. The purpose: to shame, humiliate and torment - with the bonus of a considerable financial return. The result: the demise of countless women driven to varying levels of insanity or even suicide by the evil, callous actions performed by the twisted inhabitants of apartment 6234. The victims who managed to live with themselves after their exposure, were left broken and shattered by their torment.

Ram dashed through the cavernous wall and sliced through the hand of the woman with the shotgun, she hits the floor with a thud. Next, in a show of great agility, he jumps into the air and lands a knockout kick to the blonde-haired woman frantically trying to remove the two throwing knives from her chest. He holsters his death dealing swords and steps back, leaving Brick to complete the course of justice.

Ram watches as his partner chases the women around

their evil lair, dishing out servings of extreme and devastating damage with the help of *Penny*. The level of violence is extreme, even by Brick's standards.

Our heroes rarely share more than a few words, but none are needed for Ram to realise that this group of twisted tormentors have tugged away at something inside Brick, yanked hard on a sensitive, personal nerve or two. The death-dealer ensures each blow is designed to maim, not kill, smashing bones and flesh into gruesome pulps. Ram watches on as Brick ensures each of the five women suffer until their very last breath of air. The suffering is relentless, right up to the moment their lives slip away from the poisoned bodies.

When the judgement is finally over, the bloodbath inside the apartment resembles an explosion inside a stacked-out abattoir. Brick stands in the centre of the carnage, amongst the battered remains, heaving and panting, exhausted, yet gratified by her work.

Ram mounts his bike and nods, acknowledging the outcome of her fury. He speaks a few words, telling her that it is time to go home. He fires up his raucous engine and launches his bike through the broken window.

Ram and Brick join the dizzying heights of the city's overpass once more and roar off into the darkness of the night, leaving behind them the carnage of their actions, amidst the streaks of bright neon-light.

Every single day we witness suffering at the hands of the faceless. We see them act without conscience, without care, without fear of reprisal. They believe that they are masked, hidden behind their screens, behind the curtains of their digital lairs. They thrive on the misery of the weak, of the helpless, of the defenceless. They feed from the scraps of their chosen enemies... but there comes a time when the victims stand up and fight, when they gather their arms and stand tall.

There comes a time when those that suffer have their reprisal...

There comes a time when the faceless have their judgement.

JUDGEMENT OF THE FACELESS
BY **MATT UREN**

The Watchers Inn

By Colin A. May & Richard Warnes

The Watchers Inn

Wanting to get a taste of the surroundings, a feel of the night air, I arrive at the rendezvous an hour before we agreed. I must make sure this isn't a setup... it sure feels like one. I am too old and too long in the tooth to be walking blindly into a trap I have been too lazy to avoid.

I follow a circuitous route through dark alleys and trash ridden side streets, need to be certain I wasn't followed.

I was due to meet a woman here, but at the last hour this message lands on my desk informing me she's unable to fulfil her appointment. Instead, I have been given a password... told it would get me through the front door, along with this plain white card which arrived in the post yesterday. *Why I needed a password to get in the front door of an old, run down boozer?* It's a question which has been bugging me to the point of distraction.

The fat wad of cash I'd received - concealed inside a roasted turkey of all things - hadn't really put my mind at rest either... it was more than I have made in the last six months. Whoever this mystery client is, he or she has money... or at the very least, know's how to get their hands on it.

The turkey? That was the best meal I'd had in weeks.

I realised I have never really paid any attention to this part of the city before. Out of the hundreds of cases slapped on my desk over the years, not one of them has ever brought me down here.

Most of the buildings in area are in a state of general disrepair, especially the neighbouring warehouses which are mostly boarded up and have probably been abandoned for years - yet this small pocket of the city is remarkably clear of the street trash typically littering the city.

I mean, that's trash of all kinds, but predominantly human trash: homeless, washed out down and outs huddled under giant sheets of sodden cardboard and tatty old newspapers. I do feel for them, it's not their fault society has cast them aside. Then there's the stinking drug dealers and their bottom-feeding junkies. Then you got the pro's, like that damn...

No...

No time for that now.

None of them are anywhere to be seen, as if a storm has come and flushed them all away.

That's what strikes me the most.

Well... good riddance to them.

Perhaps I should think about relocating here? The area around my office is a forsaken hole and it chokes the life from me every-single-day.

I wait just beyond the feeble beam of light cast by one of the sporadic, barely functioning lamps overhead. Strange that all the lights here are working, usually it's one in three at best in this city.

My fedora and trench coat keep me reasonably warm and somewhere near to dry, despite the soft but persistent, perfectly vertical blanket of rain.

With my choice of clothes and the horrendous weather as my ally, it's easy to blend into the darkness.

I surveyed the meeting point: a slightly odd, very old two-storey building with dark wooden framework and a grimy grey facade, wedged between two foreboding, featureless industrial units.

Two men walk confidently towards the entrance, their movement is just one notch up from a leisurely stroll, but not hurried.

They look like two old factory workers, fresh off whatever shift they've just pulled. Both dressed in matching grease-stained overalls, sturdy work boots and woolly hats. Machinists, or engineers of some-kind, maybe?

It's too dark and the distance too great to make out anything else, no matter how much I squint.

Twenty yards from the place and the door opens before them. Two almost identical men step out and walk away in the opposite direction. The door slams shut behind them, denying entrance to the factory workers.

The four men never even glance at each other, never acknowledge one another's presence.

The departing pair tuck their chins into their collars and shuffle away into the night.

The factory workers step up to the pub door and rap quietly on the beautifully rustic panel.

A slot appears almost instantly - dim light spilling out over them. They lean in close, but I am too far away to hear what is being said, I assume this pair are known, *maybe they too know the password?*

The door opens just wide enough to admit entry and they slide in.

Two in, two out, perhaps?

Another twenty minutes pass...

It's nearing the time for me to approach.

The rain has begun to work through the tiny weaves and seams of my coat, the cold is starting to kick in too. It's a miserable night for a walk.

I shuffle my way down the street, keeping far enough away on the opposite side of the road and out of any direct light.

I remain incognito until the time feels right, I then casually step out into the exposure of the streetlamp. The sloshing of water fills the air as I wade through the murky pools of rainwater gathering on the road.

I want them to see me approach, but not to know I had been standing around in the shadows, watching... waiting.

Got to act casual, got to be cool.

It's an awkward dash through the rain, I feel like I'm paddling through these pools.

I need to be calm - I'm just like any other person with a distaste for damp weather.

As I near, the door opens and a guy in a black trench coat and fedora steps out.

He sparks up a cigarette and strolls off into the cold, wet night.

He never made eye contact, never even glanced my way.

I don't understand...

The first rule of a private detective is 'there are no coincidences', but this is a massive coincidence.

I don't turn back, I keep focused...*can't get distracted, they'll notice, someone will notice.*

My client had mailed me the money-turkey to my own

apartment, not the office... they knew where I lived!

My suspicions are mounting rapidly, alarm bells are ringing here... *old habits die hard.*

Perhaps my mind is just too suspicious and the guy in the almost identical clothing to mine is just an insane coincidence which I needed to ignore... *one of two though, the four guys before me shared similar mysteries.*

The more I think about it, the more it fries my brain, not a distraction I need, got to be alert.

I step up to the door and knock: a quick rat-tat-tat, as my client has instructed.

The slot opens... no view inside.

The whole opening fills by a pair of bushy grey eyebrows.

'Whadd'ya want, buddy?' responds a gruff barking tone.

'A drink of course, it's chucking it down out here!' The slot slams shut.

Perhaps I should stick to the script?

I knock again.

The slot flicks open, once again revealing the eyebrows.

'Whadd'ya want?' the voice repeats.

I recite the bizarre phrase my client gave me, I have repeated it a dozen times or more on my journey, yet it still makes no sense to me...

'I want to swim in the sweat of a million orgies' I announce, with a guise of confidence.

The slot closes again.

An uncomfortable pause drags by before the door opens a little.

I slide through the gap sideways, hoping this is my cue to enter.

I'm damn lucky not to lose any fingers as the heavy door slams shut behind me.

I turn to face the bushy, grey eyebrows and amazed to see they're attached to the face of a woman, *I never would have guessed that!*

She can't be much over five-foot tall, hunched over slightly, it makes her appear even shorter.

She grunts and groans like a hungry beast and drags a wooden stool away from the door.

She barks at me, again in her strange husky voice, asking me why I seemed so confused... *got to think on my feet.*

'I haven't seen you in a while,' *perhaps I can bluff my way through this confrontation with a smile...* although I feel it's closer to an uncomfortable grimace.

The last thing I want is to cause trouble here, I can't afford to stand out - after all, I have no idea what this place is and if experience has taught me anything, it is to always be wary of unfamiliar surroundings.

She starts to gargle, there's words beneath the noise, she's telling me how she has been sick and how a guy named Joey had been covering her shifts - much to his displeasure... she doesn't have many nice things to say about Joey...I have no idea who either of them are.

Her rants are interrupted by a rough, nauseating, coughing outburst - the sound of her hacking up phlegm only adds to her seemingly unpalatable charms.

The barrel laugh I return as I mutter the name *Joey*, seems to crack a smile on her tough, petulant looking face, but... it could just be wind.

Damn, she really is rough looking, to put it delicately.

I take my time walking to the bar, soaking up the archaic decor of the boozer. Old photographs printed on paper mounted in shiny brass-framed glass proudly hang from the walls. Each picture depicts a totally different era of the city, *an era before the violent times I was born into, perhaps?* The pictorial views of the docks don't seem far removed from what we see today, but the docks... they never really seem to change.

The carpet is made from a kind of woven material of old, predating my limited knowledge of furnishings.

A collection of glass tankards dangle from the ceiling, each one glowing from the warm lighting nesting above.

Tables and chairs, fashioned from old, dark wood furnish the room... *where did they find all this wood?*

I have never seen a pub this quiet before, it is eerily quiet. It isn't quite ghostly, more a quiet as in calm, respectful. There are no drunks shouting and screaming. No music blasting my eardrums. No foul language and obscenities being hollered around the room. No strange old drunk guy sleeping it off in the corner.

I examine the clientele further.

Everyone quietly sits at their tables, keeping their chatter amongst their present company, discussing their business in a pleasant and polite manner. A few others sit at the bar, in their own tranquilities, just as well behaved as their fellow patrons... *this place truly is an anomaly.*

The bar stretches the breadth of the room - another construction of dark-wood, finished with highly polished brass-fittings and old-style hand pumps.

The bar-top is littered with a parade of bar mats from around the world. Some of the mats look to be older than me... and almost certainly older than the small, young lady behind the bar pulling the pints... she looks barely old enough to work, let alone serve alcoholic beverages to the subdued clientele. She is a sight for sore eyes though, an old cliché I'm not too proud to use.

Beneath the feted odour of damp clothes created by the leaky sky outside, an old familiar smell floods the air - a musty, yet welcoming aroma fills my nostrils. I suck it in, embracing it.

I order my usual tipple: a whisky on the rocks, but as my wandering eyes inadvertently examine the wide selection of ale on offer, I immediately regret my decision.

The pretty barmaid makes small talk about the ghastly weather and her plans for the days ahead.

Her face glows with a carefree happiness which is such a rarebit in this world... I almost forget to respond. I'm lost in her chirpy, warm persona.

I manage to string a few sentences together to engage the conversation, being cautious not to give anything about myself away.

During the short time spent at the bar, I have one eye on the barmaid, looking attentive to her meaningless, yet genuinely polite conversation and one eye scanning the mirror behind her, keeping a constant watch on my surroundings.

A thirsty patron interrupts the conversation to request a refill... I quietly, gratefully, slip away to a table in the corner.

The caramel coloured beverage, hidden amongst the glass

of ice, warms me down to my gut, the taste compliments its strength.

It's almost a feeling of bliss as I remove my soaked coat clinging to my body.

I sit quietly with my back to the wall, observing the movements of the room from beneath the dripping brim of my hat. My clothes which once sheltered beneath my coat are also saturated, clinging to me like they are covered in glue, yet I feel comfortable somehow, my surroundings are unusually calming… It's nice here!

This city is a breeding ground for chaos, it thrives on misery, on pain.

People scurry around the vast metropolis, consumed by all the madness, lost in their digital worlds, heads down, eyes locked onto their communicators. They avoid eye contact, evading civilities as they bump into one-another, fighting their way through the heavy swarms on the streets.

This place is different though… this pub, this boozer, this quiet little building tucked away between two run-down monstrosities, it defies the standard of living I have witnessed throughout my days.

There's a sign above the bar that reads: *The Watchers Inn*.

This is the place alright… this is where my contact told me to come, it just feels so strange… so alien.

In my head, I'm on my back foot, watching the exits and keeping my guard up, there's an uneasy feeling in my gut.

I don't want to be cornered if trouble starts, but I also want to see it coming, so I keep my eyes wide open and keep busy watching my surroundings… yet, I am comfortable, at ease at my solitary table.

I struggle to accept the serenity enclosed by these archaic walls.

I observe the hands of an interestingly ornate clock, juddering with every painful, incremental movement. I have always been a man of patience, it is a quality which keeps me in work as a private detective, a quality which helps pay the never-ending stack of bills stuffed into my mailbox each day, so I utilise the skill to remain discreet.

I continue to wait for my contact to make an appearance,

even though time is dragging its heels, I keep my cool and do my best to stay quiet and blend in.

I reach a conscientious hand into my coat and check my medicine is in the pocket.

The doctor told me they'd keep my comfortable, buy me added time... they certainly helped to comfort me, but the added time? That is something I take with a pinch of heart-rotting salt.

The woman at the door sits reading a book now, lost deep in its pages, she's a lot more pleasant when she's silent. I try to make out the cover of the book, but my eyesight fails me.

The bar's patrons continue to talk amongst themselves quietly, almost mumbling, keeping the room filled with an indistinct murmur as they gently savour their beverages.

No one seems to have taken any notice of me, no one is paying me any special attention, but I can't just assume my presence here is completely unnoticed. I can't assume I am not being watched.

There could be eyes everywhere... there generally is.

I visit the barmaid twice more after acquiring my first whisky. My thirst for the spirit had remained stronger than my curiosity for anything from the wide range of ales or various other drinks on offer - despite the promises I make to myself to stay off the strong stuff and keep my tired, aging brain alert. I'm not a young man, and my best days are sure as hell behind me, but I have never been a fool... and now isn't the time to become complacent.

I realise my heart is beginning to race slightly.

I need to be calm.

I need to take a breath and not worry.

I need to take care of that little sucker beating away in my chest.

Another hit of whisky slides down my throat. I take a lung-full of air, breathing slowly through my nose.

I calm myself, slow my mind... keep focused. The atmosphere warms me.

Finally, after nearly half-an-hour, a man comes towards me...

I hadn't noticed him enter the room, but he nods at me and speaks my name with confidence - *he knows who I am!*

He stands tall, perhaps close to seven feet. His frame is gangly and thin... spindly... you could almost say gaunt. He is well dressed in a dark-blue, tailored suit and black, fitted shirt. His shoulder-length ginger hair is tied back neatly into a pony-tail - a hairstyle I have always felt looked ridiculous on a man, especially this one - *he must be in his thirties and should know better!* His cheekbones are strong - bold, striking features on his face, almost sharp edged in their shape.

He sits at the table with me and thanks me for coming across town to meet him.

There's a moment of silence, it's uncomfortable.

I try to come up with a logical story in my head to explain this peculiar arrangement to the worried part of my conscience, but my imagination fails me.

He breaks the silence, tells me to be casual, but also to hurry-up and finish my drink.

I don't hesitate... I knock it back and place the glass carefully, respectfully, on the dark-wood table in front of me.

'What is this place?' I speak at a volume close to a whisper.

He ignores my question and signals me to follow him.

I can't say he has eased my worries, but I cautiously comply.

We walk to a door at the back of the room and he enters a key-card into a discreet slot which is almost impossible to see.

The door elegantly slides open with a gentle swoosh - it immediately occurs to me this door is the only modern thing I've seen since I entered, everything else about this place is just so alien, as if it had been taken right out of an old movie, one long forgotten.

Claustrophobia kicks in as we step into a small room and the door shuts behind me.

Small spaces are not my friend.

I need to get out of here, fast!

My heart pounds hard inside my chest and I clutch my coat.

My fingers turn white under the pressure, I am thinking

about my pills.

For the first time I am truly nervous, apprehensive about what I am letting myself in for.

Within seconds my prayers are answered, the door reopens in another gentle swoosh.

The movement has an elegance to it, one which takes my brain away from the moment... *I wish the door to my office would operate in the same manner, rather than the eerie creak and a heavy bang as it catches gusts of wind...*

I refocus my mind.

The old-worldy bar had vanished.

Instead, a bright room of bustling activity opens in front of me. It's an office of sorts, filled with sophisticated holographic screens operated by a gabble of busy techno-wizards in headsets.

This computer stuff isn't my bag, but even a moron can see whoever I was meeting is part of a well-funded and tightly organised operation.

The gadgets and gizmos on display amaze me, I can't begin to fathom how it all works.

We walk through the room, passing desk after desk of people frantically punching away at screens. A sterile smell looms in the still air. Every surface seems to be spotlessly clean.

It feels like it should be freezing cold, but it isn't, it's comfortable, an organised, busy calm.

We reach an unmanned station and my escort finally introduces himself: *Gerald Z-3463*... this is the name he palms me off with, I can't fathom why... I don't question it.

Another awkward silence for long minutes seems to pass between us as he taps away at a vibrant floating screen in front of him. He seems to be completely oblivious to my wandering, curious eyes.

A deep sigh leaves my lungs as I exhale some of my tension.

I can feel my heart slowing, but not to a regular, tranquil pace... I still have my guard up.

I try again to take as much of the room in as I can: it's a hive of extraordinary technology controlled by frantically busy geeks, zipping through endless video feeds from around the city.

They're watching everything.

They're watching us all.

Cameras are everywhere... Street corners, roads, inside properties, homes, businesses, personal communication devices. Many are in plain sight. Many more are hidden from the average person's unsuspecting eye.

I cannot believe my eyes.

The more I look around, the more I witness the scale of this mass-surveillance operation.

They have access to every camera connected to the online world, it's a vast web of voyeurism which is completely under the radar.

No, stop!

Stop staring, be professional... focus!

Don't be a fool.

Don't draw attention to yourself.

Act normal.

Act like this is nothing unusual.

I fix my boggled head and return attention to my contact.

The next few minutes go by in a blur of information-overload. My lanky contact talks at me, firing a cargo-load of information my way at a million miles-an-hour. *This man can talk. His brain seems to be working at ten times the rate of mine.*

I struggle to latch onto many of his words... the ones I do catch make no sense.

He tells me he is part of a secret organisation and he has brought me into their secret HQ. It's like a spy movie, only to my eyes... much darker.

They are privately funded, operating outside the law, outside of the grasp of the government, yet they subcontract them... and to anyone else with deep enough pockets to finance the services of him and his colleagues.

They call themselves...

The Watchers.

They have the resources to access any surveillance system throughout the city and even beyond. Not just cameras, but data logs too, but all of it only upon request.

Gerald tries to add some sort of moral standing to it all by stressing they can only operate under strict rules, ones which can never be broken. He tells me they hack into systems, both corporate and personal. *There seems to be no limits to their capabilities.*

Then, things turn more sinister and even more bizarre.

He talks of an army of super-soldiers... men and women brought back from the dead. Soldiers who are almost invincible - killing-machines, ready to be dispatched by The Watchers, but only upon the request of the client and furthermore, only with the authorisation from a small committee who govern this organisation.

The soldiers work in secret, not even knowing themselves what their purpose is - they just get issued orders and receive the appropriate abilities to perform their missions.

Their gifts are for their missions only. 'These powers are just as easily taken away as they are gifted,' he assures me.

Not all cases result in a soldier being utilised, that comes at a very high-price, one many cannot afford and one most don't deem necessary.

Gerald tells me that although as a Watcher he sees many crimes, many truly awful things - he is only allowed to investigate and act on the ones he has been assigned to... this rule stands for every operator in the room.

If an investigation leads them to witness something another Watcher is working on, it is to remain a secret, no information is shared amongst them.

'These are the rules,' he says.

I don't understand them, any of them.

Then the mood turns real dark... pitch black like the void in my blown mind.

He tells me, he has broken the rules....

Gerald says he knows who I am, what I do to pay my bills and how much money I have in the bank.

He knows where I live and he knows all about my nasty habit of drinking myself to sleep at night, wallowing in half a bottle of my favourite brand as the darkness closes in.

He knows my past... *and he probably knows my future by*

the sounds of it!

He shows me glimpses of myself on the screen.

I watch on in bemusement as I carry on my ignorant life, oblivious to the eyes of The Watchers.

Next, he shows me a video of a man meeting with a government official, Gerald doesn't discuss the particulars of the scene, but I recognise this political figure and the man whom he meets with... but it is not the shady, secretive meeting that Gerald wishes me to see...

It's the next clip which truly haunts the Watcher.

The camera records the conversation between the two men, but in the background of the shot, a child, a baby, thrown to his death from a rooftop by a pale-skinned woman, dressed in familiar gang colours.

I've seen the colours many times before... a low-level street gang who predominantly involve themselves with the distribution of illegal firearms, amongst many other criminal activities. The gang are often involved in disputes of territorial control. The woman on the rooftop wears the stripes of a lieutenant, an enforcer. *This is a new low for these guys.*

Gerald enlightens me with the specifics of the woman and her daily routines. He tells me how she has been ordered to clear the tenants out of a collective of properties and in particular: one which was once a home to the now deceased babe.

Gerald tells me the background of the murdered child... I do not wish to know, I feel sick to the stomach, but the detective in me listens anyway.

He tells me the exact location I see on the screen, but he didn't need to, I knew it all too well - there had been a handful of cases which had seen me wander into that part of the city before, it had always been a real nasty part of town.

He tells me everything he knows.

He tells it all... I still don't want to know...

...and then...

... he tells me the danger he has put me in.

To investigate anything other than what is requested and required is an offence... an offence which does not go unpunished - but most importantly and damn unluckily for me, it does not go unnoticed… ever.

His superiors have been on to him from the start, they knew about his investigation., his blatant disregard for the rules.

They knew about the baby and the female gang banger.

Now they sure as hell know about me… but they did not know what Gerald intended to do next… until now.

'They know you're here. They know you have seen this now. Everything I access here, they see. Now you have seen it, I want you to do the right thing. You have only minutes to get out of here,' he tells me.

A lump in my throat lodges hard and restricts my breathing, I try to swallow it down, but it just won't budge - it twists and contorts but it is lodged good.

I shake my head in sheer disbelief.

I stare at Gerald, examining him. I believe him to be a shy, kind man, one who strays away from conflict and drama, certainly not a fighting man.

My theory is confirmed as he begins to whimper, breaking, buckling under the pressure.

I want to hit him with the chair I am perched on, but I realise it would be a waste of energy and more importantly, a waste of time.

He is not only sealing my fate, but also his own….

They'll be coming for him too.

My heart is stuttering, beating erratically.

I reach for my coat, dumped in a wet heap on the floor.

I scramble for my pills in a messy confusion of twisted fingers, lost in their frantic search.

I find them, take two and try to calm my breathing…

…count to ten.

I force out the strength to talk and ask him: 'Why... why me?'

'I could no longer live with the burden. I relive the scene in my head every day. I really need help... I need your help,' he pleads.

His words continue to fill me with rage.

I'm distracted by movement in the corner of my eye.

I clock three armed men entering the room at the far end -

they may not be here for me, but I am not about to sit around idle, waiting for the moment of confirmation. Each second I procrastinate, is a second closer to my demise.

As I spring from my chair Gerald grabs my arm and pulls me back. He hands me an access card.

'Please, the door we came in from is an elevator with access to the roof, you must go.'

He then sinks in his chair, whining in a ball of snot and quivering tears.

I want to feel sorry for him, for what he has witnessed, for what inevitably comes next for him... but the same fate is now heading my way and by the muscle load... he is the only person I can blame.

I snarl at the blubbering man and head for the door.

I dash through the busy computer room, scanning the observant eyes of the operators as they begin to take notice of me...*damn!*

Perhaps they won't notice me access the elevator? Perhaps this is all a lie? Perhaps I am losing my mind?

I whip my head round and check to see if I am in safe distance of the guards before I enter.

The doors close and I make my way to the roof.

The elevator ride is over before I know it and the door opens.

I notice immediately that the rooftop is littered with an array of cameras, all seemingly looking at me.

I curse Gerald under my strained breath.

'Why me?' I ask myself... my brain doesn't reply.

My heart stutters again, interrupting the rhythm of its routine beat.

Pain shoots through my chest.

I wince, slam my fist into my chest.

I need my pills to kick in... *they're taking their damn time!*

I reach for the pill box in my coat again, check the bottle to see if I had grabbed the laxatives this morning by mistake.

Then it hits me...

Gerald has been watching me for days, if not weeks. He has carried out his own investigation on me. He knows my combat background. He also knows about my condition. He knows I went to the hospital last week and the good lady-doctor gave me just months to live.

He knows my fate is already sealed.

He knows… I am a dead man walking.

Gerald has reached out to me because, despite his army of undead soldiers, despite his technology, he is helpless to right the wrong that haunts him.

He is soon to be a dead man.

His employers will punish him just for investigating the unassigned case.

He needs someone like me.

He needs someone who has training… someone who has lost their purpose in life.

My end is in sight and I can almost taste it.

There is nothing I can do to stop death coming to me… but Gerald Z-3463 has reached out to me and asked me to act.

He is asking me to give a damn…

…to make my final days count.

Die a weak old man with a dodgy heart… or die trying to right a heinous wrong.

My brain frantically processes the magnitude of the operation hidden beneath the façade of the old boozer. The scale and power of The Watchers is daunting, chilling, beyond anything I have ever witnessed… ever imagined.

Gerald is asking me to die trying to avenge little Harley Eadel, an innocent child thrown to his death for being born in the wrong part of town.

My attention snags and refocuses as the elevator door behind me closes… I know it is only a matter of minutes before it reopens, filled with a team of assassins out to enforce their rules.

They will want me silenced.

They will want me gone.

I look across the rooftop to a neighbouring building, the jump must be just over fifteen feet, with maybe a six-foot drop.

The jump could possibly be achievable by a fit, healthy

man… but a big risk at my age, not to mention my condition.
I tense up, contemplating my next move.
I pause and look at my pill box.

My body goes numb and I ask myself:

'Well… how are you going out, Francis?'

THE WATCHERS INN
BY **CLAIRE RACKHAM**

FOR EMILY

YOU HAVE BEEN MY ROCK
I AM HONOURED TO HAVE YOU BY MY SIDE
X